The Creole Son

by

Roy LeBlanc

ISBN: 978-1-7349226-2-2

This book is printed on acid-free paper.

Printed in the United States of America

1

WHILE WATCHING A MARDI GRAS parade on Saint Charles Avenue, I became separated from my carefree friends. Too young to drive home I walked to the end of the parade route to catch the Canal-Cemeteries bus home. On that crowded bus, was the most beautiful Creole girl I had ever seen. She was sitting alone about three seats behind me. Lacking in confidence, I said nothing. Our eyes met, she smiled and eventually exited the bus. For the past thirty-five years not a week goes by that I do not think about that brief encounter. Memories and remorse can be like that. They have a way of becoming prisons of regret, punishment without crime. I have come to terms with these lingering ghosts of missed opportunity and moved beyond bitterness with knowledge that I am lucky and although at the end of the day, I may not have gotten very far, it is certainly a wild trip worth remembering.

Creole kids never had much luck anyway. "Dreams were reserved for rich kids living on the Lakefront. Here in the 9th Ward the best you could expect was a job and a hard hat." I was told to accept my station in life with dignity. "Dreams are a waste of time, why fish in flood water? You never catch anything and if you do it's too fucking polluted to eat anyway." These shit poor New Orleans neighborhoods were quicksand, no way out. Never the smartest, best looking or strongest, my single advantage was a back against the wall ability to work, fight harder, and take punishment better than any opponent, traits learned growing up and surviving on New Orleans streets. I acquired self confidence, kindness and generosity from loving grand-parents, suspicion and distrust from a disinterested and dysfunctional family, and an understanding of human nature from a rich variety of unique experiences gained growing up here.

I eventually learned to hide my Creole heritage behind blue eyes that I inherited from my Dutch mother, and to disguise a rough upbringing behind a thin veneer of culture and education. With success came breakfast in the Governor's Mansion, private jets, financial security the honor of being the youngest person ever elected to a major office in Louisiana, and the unfortunate distinction of having the shortest political career ever, a real Greek tragedy, some would say, but victory was sweet since success was so unexpected. When it was all said and done, I longed to reclaim many things I thought I wanted to leave behind. Life became an airport layover, not at my destination and not home either, just somewhere in between.

Back then, New Orleans was a great place for kids, like me, seeking adventure and excitement. At the Orleans Avenue pumping station, giant arms would sweep across the iron grates protecting the pump intakes. Urban refuse would be swept clean and deposited along side, usually useless trash like old tires and rusting shopping carts. Sometimes we found real treasure like the WWII GI helmet that I still have. Sitting along the levee, we used bicycle ball bearings as sling shot ammunition to shoot mullet swimming in the drainage canals. What mullet we hit, we then used as bait for the crab traps that we set along the Lake Pontchartrain Seawall.

We collected returnable soft drink bottles that were easy to find discarded around City Park and worth a nickel each. At the Bayou Road grocery, we could get two donuts for a dime. The screen doors performed valiantly keeping flies out but many still found the donuts that were displayed in open air racks. Live chickens were stacked in small metal cages along the sidewalk. Maw Maw Dupree would carefully look them over and make her selection. They called the butcher Khrushchev because he resembled the then current Russian leader. Khrushchev would open the cage and remove an unfortunate chicken. A few minutes later, he reemerged with a cleaned bird wrapped neatly in brown freezer paper, weighed the chicken on a porcelain scale, and then handed the package to Maw-Maw Dupree.

Maw Maw and Paw Paw Dupree lived through the Great Depression of the 1930's and learned a distrust of bankers. Paw Paw Dupree would cash his L&N Railroad paycheck at the Union Passenger Terminal and bring home cash. Each month Maw Maw Dupree and I would ride the Esplanade public service bus downtown to pay the bills and 'trade.' She never learned to drive nor owned a car, but was always dressed in her Sunday best. We walked to the Light Company, Water Company and Gas Company paying monthly expenses with the cash that she carried in a small coin purse. We ate lunch at the Woolworth Soda Fountain on Canal Street that carried original Italian Cream Sodas and good burgers and we window shopped at Gus Meyer's, Krauss, D.H. Holmes and Maison Blanche department stores. If we actually purchased anything it would have been from the Maison Blanche Annex on a side street behind the main store. They carried out of date clothing, damaged goods, and other discounted items.

Before heading home, we walked from Canal Street to Decatur Street over to the French Market passing the Morning Call where we shared a twenty five cent order of beignets and then inspected the farmer's produce and seafood market. Today, the Market is a tourist trap along the river near Jackson Square with tee shirt shops, restaurants and souvenirs made in China. The old market was a two or three block long open air structure with a roof supported by elaborate wrought iron pillars built during French colonial days and paved with grey flagstones deeply grooved by the passage of time and footsteps that were once used as ballasts in French and Spanish sailing ships.. The French Market was similar to bazaars that I imagined in a place like Morocco or described in tales of Ali Baba and *One Thousand and One Nights*, one of my favorite books. Creole fishermen and trappers, truck farmers, a Voodoo Priestess, and a Creole lady who sold homemade pralines rented designated spaces to display and sell their goods. Most people kept the same spot for years.

Tables were full of fresh tomatoes, alligator pears, turnip greens, and mirlitons. Each farmer sang out in a unique way, attempting to attract customers as they walked by. "Produce, Produce", "Fresh Fruit, get your fresh fruit", "Fruit Man". In the fall, we bought pumpkins and in the summer we sampled the best sliced watermelons from the back of large trucks, beds lined with straw. Maw Maw Dupree stopped at the same venders each time, purchased what was necessary and sometimes I got a free apple to enjoy on the bus ride home. When we passed near the Voodoo table we always made the Sign Of The Cross and walked quickly. Afterwards, Maw Maw Dupree blessed my forehead with holy water that she carried in a small glass bottle and we recited the "Our Father" for good measure.

The seafood market was only a few steps away but presented the senses with a completely different experience. Live crabs were kept in bushel baskets and crawfish were kept in fifty pound burlap sacks and packed so tightly that even minimal movement was nearly impossible. If you poked the sack with a stick, maybe you could see a claw move. Close inspection revealed the tiny bubbles that emitted from their mouths when out of water for any length of time. "Never eat the straight tails," Maw Maw Dupree said. A straight tail meant that the crawfish was already dead before boiling.

Each booth contained tiled tables loaded with ice that melted quickly in New Orleans summers, water drained into tiny trenches carved into the flagstones, and then flowed out to the street. The fishermen wore overalls, rubber boots, thick gloves, and carried sharp knives on their belts. Cats loved the fish market and were adopted by grateful fisherman as rodent hunters. The adopted cats watched lazily over activities from safe perches above the action. Fish were cleaned on the spot in a matter of minutes, cleaning was an art form. The rich abundance of swamps and wetlands around New Orleans was on display, from nutria skins to redfish, trout and eel. Eventually Gentilly Woods and the Carrolton Shopping Center opened promising to modernize the way New Orleans shopped. The old market had no chance competing against air conditioning, florescent lighting, parking lots and frozen foods. Everything changes!

As an affordable gift for my sixth birthday, Dad and I rode the streetcar from Carrollton down St. Charles to Canal Street and back. We stopped at Tulane University and walked the campus. He pointed out the significant buildings, their names and ages, the subjects taught in each. To a six year old, the library was overwhelming in it size. He pointed to the auditorium, "That building is where Tulane gives degrees, it is the most important of all," I remember him saying. He was runner-up in a Holy Cross High School scholarship contest, only a few points behind the award winner. Consequently, Dad would end up at a public high school, then Delgado Community College. He had planned to marry his high school sweetheart, but she crushed his spirit, "I want to marry a doctor," she told him unexpectedly one evening. He never saw her again.

2

MY MOTHER'S FAMILY WAS BAPTIST while my father's family was Creole Catholics. Paw Paw Dupree spoke fluent Creole French and some English; my father used French very seldom and then only when angry. I was forbidden from learning the Creole language since it was considered an anchor holding the lower class down. We attended Mt. Olive Baptist Church on Wednesday evenings, St. Josephs Catholic Church on Sunday mornings, and I had Catechism every Saturday. I loved the potluck dinners offered in the Mt. Olive Fellowship Hall on holidays and loved singing the traditional spirituals such as; "Amazing Grace" and "Rock of Ages." I remember Maw Maw Dupree doing her daily chores singing "Just a Closer Walk with Thee" as she moved around the small house. She sang some lyrics and hummed others, effortlessly moving between them with a graceful ease that carried throughout the afternoon. I can close my eyes today and remember her soft melodies and feel safe and protected just as I did as a child napping in her living room.

The Baptists forbade dancing and drinking. The Catholics would drink and dance all night long at every occasion: weddings, funerals, and Mardi Gras. The Catholic priest spoke in Latin while the Baptist Preacher hurled fire and brimstone to save our souls. He believed Catholics were non-Christian because they prayed with their eyes open. Dancing and drunken celebrations are a part of the New Orleans Catholic culture, but casual sex outside marriage is considered a sin. Catholic rules had to be carefully followed or one ran the risk of spending eternity in Purgatory, a lost soul roaming the earth forever in limbo between heaven and hell. Baptists didn't dance or drink but seemed open minded about enjoying the pleasures of human sexuality. My mother became concerned when a Lutheran family moved nearby. She was afraid I would get confused.

Shortly after my younger brother became ill, my mother strayed from traditional organized religion. My brother was in and out of hospitals as my parents searched for good news. The stress placed an additional strain on finances and on my parent's relationship. When traditional medicine failed, mother turned to unorthodox spiritual healers and father turned to drinking. Mother traveled the south visiting Faith Healers while my father stayed home 'watching' over sister and me. A preacher from Mobile said that my brother's health problems were punishment for father's drinking. Mother knew where the vodka bottles were hidden. She poured out the alcohol and replaced it with tap water believing this would "remove Satan's presence" from our home and cure my little brother. Instead, a fight ensued and mother received a black eye.

Sister studied Home Economics because it was an easy path to a degree. She scolded our mother for buying older hamburger hidden under a thin layer of fresh meat. "I would never be so foolish," she said. According to her we were "common" because our cups and glasses were stored upright in the cabinets. "Dust can accumulate inside the dishes promoting diseases. They should always be upside down, for health reasons. That is a proven fact," she said. Our house was built in 1948; the cabinet bottoms may never have been cleaned. I would take my chances with upright glasses.

Sis would sit for hours staring at a television that was turned off and thought she could see ghosts. Father tried to explain that it was only the reflections of people walking around the room. "You don't have the gift!" she told him. This all turned out to be good preparation for the bizarre political characters I would encounter later.

3

ON A FOGGY MORNING, I was a front seat passenger as my mother drove along Dumain Street heading to Maw Maw Dupree's house. Seat belts were considered an unnecessary nuisance back then. We approached Moss Street and Bayou Saint John where we had the right of way with the intersecting streets. We did not see the Jaguar sedan that slammed into the passenger side of our car at a high rate of speed. I was thrown into the metal dash and windshield with great force, was dizzy and confused but noticed that the broken glass and blood created unusual and interesting patterns on the vinyl seats. I could hear my mother's screams as neighbors worked to free me from the wreck. It was not until I saw Paw -Paw Dupree's 1951 Plymouth turning the corner that I settled down. That night the local radio stations listed the names of the individuals injured in riots resulting from the Dr. King assassination. I expected to hear my name because I was injured that day.

The careless driver was a Jesuit High School student late for class and found to be at fault. He explained to the police that his brake lights were not working. He ran the stop sign because, in the fog, he did not want to be rear ended. Scar tissue formed around my right eye that repeatedly caused infection and swelling. For years, I looked like a troublemaker prone to fist fights. The Judge awarded a substantial sum of money that was set aside for my college education and entrusted to my mother for safe keeping based on her promise to do so. Soon after the judgment was signed my parents used the money to fund a home remodeling project including a new second story with two additional bedrooms, a bath, a den and they purchased a new Chevrolet. Mother justified squandering my college funds because "she was in the accident, also" and besides, "I could use one of the new bedrooms," she said.

In addition to being screwed out of my college funds, I distrusted my parents for other reasons. Every young boy should have a dog. Mine was named Prince. He was a brown mutt with a touch of black around his nose and eyes. When I rode my bike in the neighborhood Prince followed or he would sit in a wagon and I could pull him around. Prince could open the fence gate with his nose; he could dig under it or jump over. He never stayed in the yard. Clothes were dried outside on lines back then and each day Prince would roam around collecting: sheets, underwear, shirts and girdles. He dragged everything to our yard. Dad was angry about the repeated calls from irate neighbors so he cut a piece of garden hose about four feet long and used it to beat Prince. He chased him around and around the small yard until Prince grew tried and then he beat him some more. I watched from the window and could hear Prince cry, but I was powerless to help.

One day Prince was gone. Days and days I walked blocks and biked everywhere calling out his name, "Prince, Prince." Dad helped in the search and drove as I called out his name, "Prince, Prince," we covered the neighborhood repeatedly, but Prince was nowhere to be found. Sometime later I thought I saw him and ran home. My mother said I could not have seen Prince. "Why not?" I asked. "Because," she said, "Your father drove Prince across town, pushed him out of the car and drove off. Get over it!" she said.

4

AS I GREW OLDER, AT age 14, there was plenty of opportunity in New Orleans to find meaningful trouble. My friends and I got into the habit of riding our bicycles, all the way past Broad Street to the Dixie Brewery. There was a brick passage way on the first level of the ancient building then used as a drive through by customers in line picking up refilled long neck cases. On occasion, the line of thirsty patrons extended clear through to the other street. The brewery provided a tap on an interior wall where customers could drink free beer while waiting. Again and again the workers repeatedly chased us off, but the slow moving brewery men had no chance of ever catching us. Eventually they ignored us altogether and went about their business while we took advantage of free beer.

Further trouble came as a result of my friends and I who could get to Bourbon Street easily by peddling straight down Esplanade Avenue to the French Quarter where we tried unsuccessfully to sneak into Strip Clubs. The huge black men in tuxedos never allowed us to enter, but they did not discourage us from peeking in. "Old enough to w-a-n-t" and they opened the door wide revealing forbidden but alluring temptations. "T-o-o young to get!" and they slammed it shut. "Now m-o-v-e along boys." The message was delivered with a cadence unique to New Orleans that tourists love. The French Quarter porn theaters had no such doormen or restrictions. Seeing penetration close-up on the giant screen was quite a shock to us. Not as surprising however, as when the lights came on and we could see the other theater customers up close. Greg, one of my best friends at the time, thought he was getting lucky with the friendly "girl" sitting next to him. The real shock would have come if he had reached under her skirt. "But she had tits!" Greg protested in his own defense. We never went back to the theaters.

As time went on, I saw these friends less and less since my father expected me to work and contribute financially to the family. I started delivering the *States Times* after school since I was about thirteen years old. Father built a basket from scrap wood he salvaged from a construction sight and painted a lightening bolt on the side. I struggled to handle the bike and heavy wooden basket full of papers. When I turned corners, I did not have enough strength to move the handlebars back. The bike would go in a short circle then fall over. Unable to lift it, I removed all the papers, stacked them nearby, leaned the bike against a tree and replaced the papers in the basket. This happened three or four times each day. I thought my Dad built the homemade basket because it was a neat idea, not realizing we could not afford the expense of a real one.

I found that the task was easier for me to load the wooden basket only half full, deliver those papers and return to the station for the rest. The manager did not want to wait around so he began leaving the remaining papers on a street corner near my route's midway point. This system worked fine until those papers were stolen. Another hit to my financial bottom line. Paperboys were also charged for supplies including rubber bands and plastic rain bags. If it was a rainy month, profits could completely disappear. At the end of each monthly billing cycle, we received invoices, the paperboys' responsibility involved going to each customer and collect the money owed. One customer told me to "Come back when my husband is home." This went on for a time until I returned one day to discover that they moved away.

The most important day of each month occurred when I collected enough money to cover expenses, everything after that was money in my pocket, net profit. To celebrate this monthly milestone, I always went to Landry's Lakeview Restaurant and ordered a hamburger with butter and ketchup only. The waitress knew me and would announce my arrival, "Our paperboy is here, hamburger, ketchup and butter only and a crème soda coming up!" I felt like royalty because of the friendly service and the fact I was earning and spending my own money.

The newspaper manager invested in his business by purchasing a new baby blue Dodge cargo van. The vehicle was a no frills work horse that could carry dozens of paper bundles at a time. He delivered the papers to the station and was driving away when an older boy picked up a rock and hurled it towards the van's back window. As the window shattered, the van skidded to a stop. Almost in concert all the older boys said "He did it" and pointed at me. I pleaded with the angry manager, but he had witnesses and insisted on telling my father. The damage was a $110.00 dollar repair bill that my father reluctantly paid. "Are you saying that all those boys and the manager are all lying?" he asked. "Yes!" I said. The other boy's untruthfulness was a problem; the money was a problem and no one believed me. Reluctantly, I reimbursed my father each month for about one year until the bill was paid in full. The manager said he hoped I learned a good lesson from all this. I sure the hell did! I learned that I did not like getting screwed.

5

FORTUNATELY IT WAS EASY TO find work around the city and I had various "jobs" including: Professional Pallbearer, bus boy, drug store delivery boy and door to door encyclopedia salesman. All helped contribute in different ways to my developing a hard attitude and sarcastic outlook. I held the drug store job for a long time and made good money especially when accounting for tips earned from deliveries. The pharmacy was located on the corner of Esplanade and Grand Route Saint John, one of New Orleans oldest neighborhoods. The store provided bicycles that were used for delivering small dry goods orders and prescriptions. The front counter was handled mostly by attractive young school girls or older ladies. I was in the back near the pharmacist when I noticed a nervous looking customer standing off to one side. Finally, he gathered the courage and approached the counter girl. "I would like a pack of Trojans please." Condoms were kept behind the counter back then. She looked around for a while. "I don't see any Trojans but we do have Winston and Marlboro." I came around and handed him the merchandise. "It's on the house," I said.

The pharmacy closed at 9:00 PM but we began balancing out the day's receipts, counting the register, and inventory at about 8:30 PM. The door was locked at that time and we only allowed customers we recognized to come in after hours. Paul walked to the front intending to lock the doors; two men burst in, pulled stockings over their heads, and began waving chrome pistols. The narcotics and other drugs with "street value" were kept in a large safe that was time locked at 8:30 PM, it was nearly impossible to open before 9:00 the next morning. The pharmacist shut it only moments before. "Get on the floor, mother fucker! What the fuck you looking at?" Paul and I followed their instructions and lay face down with our hands behind our heads in the narrow aisle between two counters. They ignored the cash register, leaped over the counter, and headed directly for the drugs.

"Open the safe!" was repeated over and over, louder and louder. The pharmacist was too nervous to get the combination sequence correct. "Open the safe, mother fucker!" Open the safe, mother fucker!" Then shots rang out. Four maybe five, I lost count. The sound of large caliber weapons fired in a small enclosed area is unsettling. I could not see what was happening but knew if the druggist was dead the addicts would not want any lingering witnesses able to identify them. Maybe I could survive the shots until the police and medics arrived. But who was around to call them? I didn't want to be shot in the face or head and worried about living forever in a vegetative state, a burden on others. I worried about who would have to clean the mess up, if we were shot, and hoped it would not be the pretty counter girls. It is funny what you think about at times like that.

The junkies fled as quickly as they came. They had shot the safe. not the pharmacist. Of course, the safe did not open and the drug thieves left with nothing. The pharmacist was curled up in the fetal position, shaking uncontrollably, incoherent, and had defecated on himself. The incident changed me. I felt invigorated, fearless and strong. I survived. Ultimately all fear is rooted in death. I lay side by side with death and won. I met death. While death is always nearby, death no longer held any power over me. The N.O.P.D. crime lab showed up a week later to collect fingerprints. How typical of New Orleans police work.

6

I WORKED AS A BUS boy, dishwasher and janitor at the Bounty Seafood Restaurant. The Bounty was a popular seafood place built out over the lake on piers in West End, an area of many well known and popular restaurants, and bars. I worked Friday night, Saturday night, and prepared the restaurant for opening each Sunday morning. The black dishwashing crews smoked pot all night long. They worked at the end of a long corridor behind the kitchen far away from the diners. The air return vents were sealed with tape so the cloud of marijuana smoke would linger and not circulate around the restaurant.

The kitchen staff placed tiny cherry tomatoes as decorations on salads which the dishwashing crew hurled as tiny projectiles against any uninvited "preppy pussy" bus boys intruding on their domain. However, sexy, white, college girl waitresses would sneak back there at every opportunity, hike up their skirts, sit on tray stacks, take a few hits on a joint, and then slip back to the dining room. I was accepted by the dishwashers because they knew my family had roots in the 9th Ward and I shared the same last name with two of the blacks, not uncommon for French Creole families. My specific branch of this complicated Creole family tree contained descendents from Holland, explaining my unusual features with a café au lait complexion and blue eyes. In New Orleans, Creoles could easily move between white and black society so it became my job to push dish racks back and forth through out the night, never sure exactly where I fit in.

On Saturday nights I clocked out at about 1:00 am, played pinball for an hour or so with friends and was back at 7:00 am Sunday morning. When I left on Saturday night, I always placed a five gallon bucket upside-down near the kitchen light switch. I stood on the bucket because I was afraid of the rats that scurried about when the lights came on. The rats were always a problem because of the water and abundant food. The city constructed a common trash collection area with rows of large steel dumpsters enclosed behind a high wooden fence and intended to address the rodent problem. However, the so-called solution only made matters worse as restaurant workers were afraid to enter the enclosed area populated by rats bigger than raccoons. We stood outside the fence on each side of the large trash bags and simply hurled them over. Sometimes the trash bags tore open spilling the smelly restaurant waste across a wide area. Rarely did the trash bags land in the dumpsters – a monumental mess.

Spinnakers' Disco was next door and also built out over the lake with boat docks and an outdoor bar across the back of the Disco. Whenever the Bounty bus boy crew could take a break, we gawked at the yachts, speedboats, and easy looking girls coming and going. With boat names like "Sin or Swim" and "Columbian Gold," we knew what was going on. We saw girls slip their bras into their purses before getting on board and we saw boat owners buying alcohol by the case before taking on more passengers. A couple was standing together on Spinnaker's back deck looking out over the lake and sunset. She was wearing a low cut dress open and loose fitting under the arms. He reached around the dress and began foundling her breasts. Our manager promised to fire everyone if we did not, "return to work and concentrate on our jobs. You don't get pussy when you're unemployed," he said. We all looked up to him. He had an Associate Degree in Restaurant and Tourism Management, planned to open his own restaurant "at the right time" and drove a fine blue Trans-Am with a screaming eagle on the hood.

Employees from the various establishments got to know each other from frequent trips to the garbage enclosure. The Spinnaker Bar Backs, those guys that brought glasses to the bartender, said that they could "Sneak us in through a side employee entrance. Look for a white towel in the bathroom window after 1:00 AM as the signal." We brought a few pounds of boiled shrimp from the Bounty kitchen and a small amount of pot borrowed from the dishwashers as an expression of our appreciation.

The music was pounding "Do a little dance, make a little love, get down tonight"; lights were flashing brilliant colors while the strobes created a different and disoriented visual reality. Now you see it, now you don't as artificial smoke took on the colors of the alternating lights. I stood for a while in one spot trying to comprehend the dance floor scene when I was tapped on the shoulder. "You can stay right where you are. I like looking at your ass!" she said while holding my hand and moving us towards the dance floor. The flashes, strobe lights and smoke made it difficult to see what was happening but I enjoyed her hands caressing my body, foreplay disguised as dance moves. I did the same.

My buddies figured out what I was doing and started circling around like sharks hoping to share in my good fortune. My new dance partner put up with this expression of youthful exuberance for only a short while. "I'm not in the mood for a wham-bam-thank you ma'am tonight." She left in frustration. I was grabbed tightly by the arm, "Hey, punk, what did you do to my girl?" He was really big, like a football player, but had too much to drink and seemed stupid. He stood about a foot away as he pointed his finger in my chest, perfect range for me to knock his lights out. Experienced street fighters got face to face, nose to nose to prevent a surprise right hook. Not this fool. "I don't know you or your girl!" My buddies circled around cutting off his retreat route. "You think you are tough with your little gang of queers. You so bad, why don't you hit me?" he said.

I reached into my pocket for the taped up roll of quarters I carried for this purpose. When held tightly in a fist it was like throwing a punch with a sledgehammer. I got a good footing, leaned into the right hook with my entire weight and caught him completely off guard. The hit was so powerful I thought it cracked my wrist but the snapping sound came from his jaw. He stood momentarily as if nothing happened, then just collapsed onto the floor. One of my gang, Johnny, reached down, took the guy's wristwatch and "rabbit eared" him by turning his pockets inside out looking for money. As we moved around in our group, I noticed most of the men avoided any eye contact with us, many moved out of our way completely. I had grown up with these knucklehead friends, but never realized how menacing we could look with black tee shirts, gold chains and a don't-give-a-fuck attitude. I liked this feeling of respect.

7

LATER THAT SAME WEEK I answered a newspaper classified employment ad for a sales job with"unlimited earnings potential." Having never worked in the "publishing" industry, I was unsure what to expect. The first interview was in a group format where questions were encouraged. Four or five prospects were told to leave right off the bat because of how they were dressed, mannerisms, or just because.

"Is this a bullshit job selling encyclopedias?" a sleepy looking applicant asked.

"Pack your shit and leave. You're done" the trainer said. "That's right, get the hell out of here."

The applicant whispered "Fuck you" as he tried to save face while exiting the room.

"Anyone else want to leave? Do it now. If you want to make money? Stay." I needed to make money so I stayed.

Expert presenters gave the sales spiel training using multi colored posters and other props. They were well dressed and wore diamond rings and a small gold pick axe pin that indicated their ability to "break the ice" with potential prospects. Salesmen earned about $150 per sale and were expected to sell three or four sets per week. How hard could this be? After all, the parking lot looked like a Cadillac dealership displaying the latest models.

During sales training classes we learned to use posters showing high school and college graduation ceremonies. The cost for the entire book set averaged about 30 cents a day. "The cost is less than a few cigarettes or a bag of potato chips. Are your children worth more than cigarettes?" "Always look the prospect in the eye. If you can't do that, then stare at their forehead just above the eyes." They will not notice the difference, we were assured. "When shaking hands never let go first," to do so indicates weakness. After you present the "close" shut up and say nothing more. "Whoever speaks first will lose." Once you gain entrance to a home, look for the Command Module. This is going to be the large recliner in the corner with the TV remote, magazines, papers and a beer on the stand nearby. This is the center of power. The master of the home sits here. "When you walk in look for the Command Module and sit there. This will give you an important advantage over the decision maker" they taught.

On my first night out, we were driving to Port Sulfur when our team leader began giving instructions on what to do if you happen to get arrested! "This happens from time to time because of city ordinances against working people," he explained. The instructions included fake local names and out-of-town lawyers. "If you make a sale, tell the customer that the company will call tomorrow to verify the information. Tell them that you are up for a promotion and that it is very important that they give positive responses to all the questions." Every customer had the right to renege on the deal within three business days. By answering the follow-up call with positive responses, they forfeited that right.

After many unsuccessful attempts, I was finally invited into a home. The nice lady said that they had been trying to buy a set of encyclopedias from a grocery store promotion offering a different book each month. They purchased volumes A, B, and C, but missed D and E and started back with F. There were no second chances to complete the set. I noticed the Command Module in the corner with the remote control and beer can just as expected. The decision maker returned from the bathroom. "Who the hell are you?" he asked. "This nice young man is selling encyclopedias." I reached out my hand in a determined manner to shake his and did not let go. I guess I was staring above his forehead because he turned with a puzzled look towards the ceiling to see what I was looking at, still shaking hands. Finally, he pulled his hand away and turned toward the Command Module. I jumped ahead and sat in the chair while adjusting the side lever preparing to deliver my sales pitch. "Oh my" the lady said with her hand over her mouth. "No one ever sits in his chair!"

He said nothing as he opened the front door. He came back towards me, picked up my sales material, notebook and sales forms, and threw everything out the door like he was pitching a no hitter for the Yankees, "Get the fuck out!" It was a windy night and the forms blew down the street. I was barely past the threshold when the door slammed shut and porch light turned off. I collected my stuff and I decided to give it another try.

A young wife said they were planning to start a family and a purchase like this may be a good idea. Her husband recently began working offshore on oil rigs with a two-week on and one-week off schedule. She informed me that he was not due home for another week. "Would you like to watch a movie?" she asked as she opened the cabinet next to the TV. Porn flicks were arranged according to sexual positions and activities with a master index taped to the inside of the door. "Do you have a favorite position?" she asked as she described the breathe and depth of the extensive collection. She said her husband had gotten her used to "it" and she was having a hell of time adjusting to his new job schedule. I spent two weeks training to sell the encyclopedias and a month going door to door, but never earned one dime.

8

PAW PAW DUPREE WAS A Mason and he added my name to the list of professional "on call" pallbearers. The Masons provided this service to local funeral homes and charged $12.00 each per funeral. Sometimes, I could schedule three or more funerals in a week. I enjoyed wearing a suit; although I had only one suit and only one clip-on tie. Riding around town in a limousine gave me the opportunity to get to know the good natured and generous members of the Mount Mariah Masonic Lodge. Most were WWII veterans with fascinating stories of South Pacific adventures. Their lodge raised funds for Children's hospital and college scholarship programs. Paw Paw Dupree and the lodge director, Mr. Ferguson, wanted to sponsor my Masonic membership, but my father forbade it. He claimed the Masons were involved in the Kennedy assassination.

Aside from working, my father insisted on one other requirement: good grades. Nothing else mattered much. I could stay out all night, hang out in the French Quarter, drag race, drink, fight and play with the girls, "just being a boy," he said. I knew never to push him too far and learned to study just enough to earn grades satisfactory enough to keep him off my back. I was grounded from time to time and pushed around a little, but his methods of motivation were less and less effective as time went on.

I also knew how far I could push the school principal. Although I did misjudge the limits from time to time and suffered the consequences. On one occasion the principal grabbed me by the front of my shirt and pulled me out of the classroom into the hallway. "I am a Vietnam veteran" he explained as he held up his right hand and made a peace sign. He folded the two raised fingers over his thumb forming a fist with two raised knuckles. He pressed those two knuckles hard against my throat. "I can punch you like this and you will drown in your own blood. It will take weeks for them to figure out what happened to you." I looked into his eyes without blinking. "Do it!" I said. "Do it!" He let go of my shirt.

My screwed-up attitude was not entirely the school's fault, college was expensive and my parents had already wasted my education money. I was pissed about that for a very long time. Since I had no chance of going to a university I saw no real reason to excel in school. Most likely, I would learn a trade and get a job like most men in my family. However, my father seemed to believe that I had potential to be more, "maybe earn some type of college scholarship" he hoped, probably because he felt guilty about spending my college money or because he spent years working as a maintenance electrician on the campus of Tulane University.

Nevertheless, he did give in to my persistent nagging about a "real" job with "real" pay and eventually had me hired on as a union laborer at a downtown construction project. I was issued a temporary union card that was valid for three months, allowed only very specific job activities, but earned a generous $12.00 per hour. On my first day, another laborer approached and said his girlfriend could not make this month's rent. "She is sitting in that car by the gate, trying to earn extra cash. She's doing blow jobs for $25.00, a few in line ahead of you, but it's worth the wait. Best you ever had!" he said. "This is your girlfriend?" I asked with a puzzled expression. "Yeah, that's right, she's doing blow-jobs, so what? I didn't say you could fuck her!" I opened my wallet and handed him $15. "It's a donation, forget about the blow job," I said. "Andre, everybody does this; we all help each other out. You'll see."

A cement slab had been poured incorrectly on the third level of the new office tower. Access was limited to a narrow hallway just wide enough for the passage of one wheelbarrow. I spent three months breaking this stubborn slap apart with a sledgehammer, loading the chunks in the wheelbarrow and hauling the pieces out to the street. The work was hot, dusty, backbreaking work, my arms hurt, my back hurt and gloves did little to prevent calluses and blisters. My girlfriend complained about my rough hands, but I was tired and exhausted anyhow so it made little difference.

This was not the kind of tired cured by an afternoon of rest. No, I was physically bone tired and spiritually exhausted, it took all the strength I could muster just to get out of bed each morning. When I complained, Dad's only response was, "Welcome to my life." He picked up his grey lunchbox with the Perfect Circle Piston Rings sticker on the outside and a bologna sandwich and chips inside and we headed out the door. "When you work hard you don't always get ahead, sometimes all you get is more work," he said. I was beginning to think that maybe college was not such a bad idea.

9

MY GIRLFRIEND, ANGELA, SAID "IF you don't start doing better in school, then I'm not going to kiss you anymore!" We had become very friendly and enjoyed each other's company immensely. I met her after school each afternoon. Since she did not need to wait for the public service bus, we had almost an hour to park before she was expected home. She raised her Catholic school girl skirt and pulled her silky underwear to the side, "Do you want this again?" The very next day, I drove to Delgado Community College near City Park and registered for two evening classes. Entry level economics and personal finance were selected because I could fit these classes conveniently into my high school and work schedules and tuition was dirt cheap.

Registration personnel said everyone had to have a high school diploma in order to enroll for college credit courses. "Not a problem. Of course I have a diploma. Just not with me at the moment." She insisted I would need to bring a copy back no later than the following week and could complete the registration at that time. Ignoring her directions, I smiled, picked up the completed forms from her table and moved right along to the Bursar's office, paying the nominal registration fees and tuition.

When I met the college president, Dr. Craig Demarest for the first time; he shook my hand and welcomed me to Delgado, "Glad to have you." He said as he looked past me towards the growing line of students. Being a college president seemed to be a very good gig. He was dressed like a banker and had young, beautiful assistants. They politely accepted my money, gave me a receipt and a student number and asked if I wanted a photo with the college president. The high school diploma issue never came up again.

My high school grades improved dramatically and the school principal sent a letter home acknowledging this remarkable turnaround. The knuckle head friends I hung around with said I was a becoming a "pussy" because I stopped skipping out of school, drinking Jack Daniels in the school parking lot, drag racing on city streets, buying test answers, and running homework pools. Today they are brick layers, tow truck drivers, rent collectors, or felons.

Johnny and Paul were my best high school friends. Johnny decided it would be fun to burglarize Radio Shack stores. Seeking more thrills he began hitting the stores during business hours, firing at random as he entered. The Juvenile Court Judge allowed Johnny to leave the country or face unpleasant consequences here. He spent three years with relatives on the Island of Majorca off the coast of Spain. While there, he eventually got things together, finished school, returned to New Orleans, and joined the Coast Guard. He advanced quickly and was considered for an important promotion. The Defense Department background review turned-up the Radio Shack matter and Johnny's lack of honest disclosure. The Dishonorable Discharge lingers like a bad tattoo.

Paul's father was a prominent OBGYN. Paul made his first "easy" money by selling prescription pads that he found in his father's home office. Unsatisfied, he began writing fake prescriptions and selling them to street junkies in the French Quarter. He is now a convicted felon and makes a living collecting and selling scrap metal. We were the best of friends for four years, like brothers, but after graduation day I never saw or spoke to them again. The break with my two friends was like turning off a switch. At 18 years old, four years of high school seems like an eternity because it is a large percentage of our lives up to that point. As time rolls along, any single four-year time span becomes less and less significant to the total picture. Ulti-mately, we began to reminisce about entire decades, and then we die. I was beginning to excel at academics and craved the rush from win-ning intellectual competition just like I had from fist fights or drag race victories. Things change.

10

FOR MY FIRST SEMESTER AT Delgado College, I had a 4.0 GPA. Registration for the second semester at Delgado was much easier since I was now considered a "Continuing Student in Good Standing" or CSGS. I enrolled in two more Political Science classes to explore my growing interest in politics and government. Also during this time, my high school GPA eventually inched upward and upon graduation I had a worthwhile high school education and four college courses with 12 credit hours on my transcript. However, since I had squandered three years of high school, my overall grades were not strong enough for scholarship qualification. No scholarship meant no university education, so I planned to work full time, save a little money, and take a community college course here and there; maybe I was just a floodwater fisherman after all.

"Andre, this is Mr. Ferguson from the Mount Mariah Masonic Lodge."

"How are you young man? I understand you finished your senior year with nearly all A's and you also completed college courses. We are all very proud of your accomplishments." He asked about my plans for the future and college. "Did you know Mount Mariah Lodge awards a scholarship each year to a deserving student?"

"No, I did not know this," I said.

"The vote was unanimous. The scholarship is yours! It won't cover Princeton, but it will get you to a state university."

All I could say was "Thank You, Thank You, and Thank You!"

-29-

College and Campaign Victory

11

ACCEPTED AS A FRESHMAN AT the University of New Orleans or, UNO, I enrolled as a Political Science major. I was attracted to the win or lose nature of the political struggles that I studied. A politician cares about only one thing—the vote, deliver more than one vote, and you begin to wield power. For example, the best way to get a new school building constructed is to organize voters. Deliver votes at election time and in return that politician will work to build the school. Influence is earned because the voters see you as someone able to get things done and the politician sees you as someone able to deliver votes, a win-win situation. The process worked that way for Tammany Hall in New York, it worked that way for Huey Long, and it works that way today.

I searched for a way to deliver and organize votes. The "UNO College Republicans" were a small group of loosely organized weirdoes without a sponsor or effective leadership that the school planned to disband after the next election cycle. I changed my voter registration to Republican and was elected Parliamentarian of the College Republicans without opposition. As Parliamentarian I soon discovered that the new president elect of the club was not a registered voter and I let that fact be known. I became President by default.

The most effective way to get college boys into any organization is to lure them with attractive college girls. We planned bake sales with girls in tight fitting Reagan-Bush T-shirts manning the tables. The club gave away hundreds of free tee shirts. Even young Democrats were seen wearing Republican shirts; a free tee shirt is a free tee shirt. The year was 1983 and Ronald Reagan was running for re-election. The National Party was willing to fund nearly any request in an effort to organize college campuses.

I located a 25-year old dilapidated VW micro bus. Our plan was to drag the micro bus to a location on campus near the Chancellor's office. Since official permission for this caper was difficult to obtain, we had to drag the micro bus during predawn hours. Towing was challenging since the bus lacked lights, adequate brakes, and a wind-shield. Since no one had a tow bar we used rope. David Lang, a dare-devil type offered to pilot the VW. Approaching the first intersection, unable to stop and trying to avoid an impending rear end collision, David swung wide around the tow car. The momentum swung both vehicles in complete circles around each other at least twice. First, I saw the van's rear then the front then around again. Disaster was avoided only because at that hour there was no other vehicle at the intersection. "Man that was great, so cool" David was thrilled. We proceeded on at about 5 MPH after that thrill.

The van was spray painted like a Mondale campaign vehicle and for a quarter, anyone could take a swing at it with sedge hammers. "Who is responsible for this? Move it now!" The University Chancellor was in a rage. "Every one of you will be expelled", even at this distance I could see the wiggly veins on the side of his head popping out. Angela had painted "Fritz and Tits", a reference to Geraldine Ferraro, the female vice presidential running mate to Mondale. That proved to be the tipping point for Chancellor O'Leary, but since all four tires were flat or damaged there was little anyone could do. Besides the event was a huge success. Hundreds took swings and classes were disrupted.

I neglected to make arrangements to have the van removed from university property after the event. Nothing useable remained of the VW; even junk yards would not take it. Chancellor O'Leary called my house each day until the van was eventually dragged away by a scrap metal company. Mother always figured I would become a delinquent drop-out, but in a strange way I think she was impressed that I was able to upset such a powerful man. He suggested that I may fit in better at a different university and the College Republican Group should be barred from campus, "Forever!" We donated the net profits to the Chancellor's Scholarship Fund solving many problems at once.

The College Republicans were also asked to provide volunteers for local Republican candidates running for State Representative, State Senate, judgeships, local school boards and the City Council. Students manned phone banks, canvassed neighborhoods, placed yard signs, and volunteered at election headquarters. We helped a little known State Representative candidate, Robert Warner, by producing a favorable push poll. A push poll is a misleading effort by one candidate to discredit another.

Fifty or so college volunteers manned phone banks calling targeted voters. The questions were directed towards households already identified as likely Republican voters and designed to reinforce our candidate's commitment to conservative values and forge a view of his opponent as a bleeding heart Liberal. Over sixty percent of all responses were recorded as positive for our candidate. The push poll results helped Robert make a respectable showing. Although he was unable to win, the results helped him secure an important commission appointment later. This was the biggest political IOU I had earned thus far and expected to cash in on it at the appropriate time.

12

ANGELA AND I DECIDED THAT we wanted to get married. However, Dad was not pleased. "Son you only have a year of college left, why not finish school first?" he asked. Angela and I had our minds were made up. While sitting on the Lake Pontchartrain seawall, we discussed finances. "My goal is to save $4,000 dollars. With that kind of money we will be in good shape," I said. Angela looked in my direction. "How will you ever save that much money?" she asked.

We planned our wedding to be a little different and thought it would be nice to have our Dads do the readings during Mass as a way to honor them. My father was nervous about public speaking, but agreed and began practicing. Angela's father, Louie, operated an earth moving business with three old dump trucks and was uncomfortable in any social situation. His friends called him 'Pushrod.' He said he would think it over.

Pushrod was sitting at the head of the table, I was to his right and Angela sat across from me. One month before the wedding and we were enjoying a spaghetti dinner while discussing last minute wedding details. "My Dad is doing the readings, it's really not that difficult," I explained with a light hearted laugh. My future father-in-law thought I was making fun of him. He picked up a dinner knife with his right hand and jammed it into my left leg, just above the knee. The blade penetrated up to the handle. "Nobody mocks me!"

Pushrod screamed. "Nobody!" Surprisingly, I felt almost no pain, as my body filled with adrenalin and confusion, every bit of strength focused on survival and defense, although the sight of so much of my own blood was very unsettling.

We canceled the formal wedding ceremony, hoping to avoid a potential brawl and were married by the priest in his private chambers. A small reception was held in the University Center building on UNO's campus. I sold my car for honeymoon cash and we drove to Saint Augustine, Florida for a four day trip in Angela's old Mustang. I am polite to Pushrod and the families do usually get together for holidays, however the stabbing incident is difficult to overlook.

13

MY POLITICAL CAREER BEGAN, UNEXPECTEDLY
when a New Orleans City Councilman asked me a question. "Andre,
I need an intern to work at the New Orleans Council Chambers. Can
you recommend someone from your college group?" the councilman
asked.

"I would like to do that myself." The Chambers were not what I
expected, carpets were repaired with duct tape, furniture was banged
up World War II era surplus, boxes and files were crammed everywhere. Interns and secretaries sat at green metal desks directly outside
the individual council offices, wires crisscrossed the floors drawn on
power strips from single outlets. I sat at my desk, answered phone
calls and greeted visitors.

The Eastern areas of Chef Menteur and the Rigolets were in District "E" and outside the flood protection levies. Chef Menteur turns
into Gentilly Blvd. and then into Broad Street, the rest of the country knows this road as Highway 90. At one time, Highway 90 was an
important thoroughfare connecting New Orleans and the Mississippi
Gulf Coast.

A minor hurricane hit the city and flooded low lying areas inun-
dating the small bars, restaurants and fishing camps, creating moun-
tains of debris. As the councilman's representative, I was sent to a
neighborhood meeting with specific and clear instructions to discuss

cleanup procedures. "At the direction of Councilman Fourroux, please haul your debris to the road. The city sanitation department will send trucks and crews on the appointed day to take it away. City workers cannot remove trash from private property," I said reading from the Councilman's memo.

The residents did as they were told and hauled the trash onto Highway 90 awaiting city pickup as promised. The councilman did not realize that city workers could not clean a state road, due to different governmental responsibilities and agencies. The state had an obligation to open the highway as quickly as possible and arrived with bulldozers pushing debris back into the private yards. The city still refused to clean private property.

I have never seen a group of people as angry as the neighbors were at that next 'emergency' meeting. The councilman spoke first, "I know what a difficult time this has been for all of you. I am here on behalf of the Mayor's office and the City Council to apologize for this unfortunate misunderstanding. First, let me say that I accept full responsibility." A business owner shouted he could not launch boats if the road is blocked. "Please let me finish," Fourroux said. "We were all young at one time, and this is an extraordinary situation. I stand by this young man; he continues to have my confidence." He turned in my direction and placed his hand on my shoulder. "Andre meant no harm, only trying his best to help. We need to support young people like this! How many of you could have handled this type of situation at Andre's age?" He asked. "The city equipment will be out tomorrow and I will be here to personally supervise cleaning up this mess." At the meeting's end people came over and thanked me, many thought I had a great future ahead in politics. "Never trust a politician." Dan Planchet was a lawyer from the Vieux Carré area representing storm victims. "Those bastards will screw you every time. If you run for office give me a call." He handed me his card with his personal direct line written in pen across the top. "Maybe I can help," he said.

I was interested in a career in politics, but shocked that the Councilman would blame me for his incompetence. After working so hard to help constituents, I was publicly embarrassed and blamed for problems I had sincerely tried to solve. Fourroux put on a great performance as he pulled his chestnuts out of the fire by sacrificing mine. The realization that I was an expendable pawn and not the valuable team member I imagined was a real Santa Claus moment, shattering my self perception and naïve views of political purpose. What hurt most was the truth, I was expendable, a convenient lackey.

14

ENCOURAGED BY THOSE COMMENTS, I became an enthusiastic candidate for the Orleans Parish Republican Executive Committee (PEC). This is an insignificant chicken shit office winnable with only a small budget. But it was interesting to me because my name would be printed on official ballots and I could become a real 'elected official.' I focused on a few important facts that made PEC especially appealing to me as a political stepping stone. First, The National Republican Party would hold their 1988 National Convention in New Orleans. The Republican PEC would do much of the planning and organizational work. Second, elected members of the committee had Orleans Parish parole power, really cool!

Persons arrested on any municipal charge and held at the Orleans Parish Prison (OPP) could be released with a simple phone call from a PEC member. I would most likely be the only college student in America who could have friends released from jail. All I had to do was call Orleans Parish Central Lockup, give my name and say, for example, I want Johnny Boudreaux released. It was done. This presented more opportunities to earn political IOU's.

The Vieux Carré lawyer, Dan Planchet, contributed to my PEC campaign and paid for mailings and newspaper ads, assuring an easy victory since no other candidates spent any money. "An investment in the future," he said. On occasion he would call "Andre, I'd like you to parole someone," he would give me a woman's name. "She was arrested for loitering at a French Quarter hotel," Dan said. I knew he worked in the Vieux Carré and usually at night, but I certainly did not know anything more and did not want to know anymore. A newspaper reporter asked why I was paroling prostitutes and who was paying me! I never paroled anyone arrested for prostitution. "Loitering? Yes. Prostitution? Never!" I said. "I haven't received anything other than legal campaign contributions from anyone." I told the reporter. Dan said his investment was, "already paying dividends."

Parole Power provided an entree into aspects of New Orleans usually hidden like French Quarter courtyards. Dan Planchet owns an apartment on Magazine Street above his favorite art gallery and a home in the Lakeview area with views of the Municipal Yacht Harbor. He wears seersucker suits and white shoes during the summer. As a Zoo Board Member, he organized the annual Zoo To Do for fifteen years, the highlight of the city's social season.

Dan's philanthropic accomplishments were topped when he spearheaded a successful city-wide campaign to raise taxes supporting the arts in public schools and construct a new school dedicated to that purpose. The girls he represented worked in the most expensive hotels and catered to needs of traveling businessmen and politicians, providing female companionship. The girls drove expensive Italian convertibles, consulted Financial Advisors about their brokerage accounts, and obtained college degrees. Dan said clients would fly across the country for a few hours with a Louisiana Creole girl.

15

DAN ENCOURAGED ME TO LOOK around for greater opportunity and suggested he would help fund my political ambitions. I thought about running for the New Orleans City Council District "A" seat. Council District "A" was the only New Orleans district where a Republican had any chance of winning. District A included the Uptown and University areas as well as Lakeview Lake Vista and Lakeshore. The 9th Ward was the poorest and controlled by NWAC (Ninth Ward Action Committee) organization. The 7th Ward was middle class and included much of the Creole sections of New Orleans and parts of Gentilly and run by the LIFE organization. Blacks and Creoles were always in disagreement. The other districts fell into line supporting one or the other. Therefore, Council District "A" became the swing vote, deciding many important issues. Individual wards, except for the Wards that contained Council District A, had their own political organizations. Like politics in the Tammany Hall style, if you belonged to the organization and your candidate won, jobs and other rewards were handed out like candy.

You needed their endorsements, you went before their boards to get their endorsement, but the candidate had to pay a pro-rata share of their advertisement.

If you totaled what they received in pro-rata share from all the politicians, the total exceeded the amount spent on advertising. The excess was used within the ward as favors to buy votes through

Popeye's dinners, Groceries, and Rides to doctor. Of course, rides to the voting booth was assumed.

Dan told me the story of Keith Hayes, a driver "Wheel Man" for Ninth Ward Action Committee (NWAC). . During election qualifying time four years earlier, Keith drove NWAC candidates back and forth to Baton Rouge as they qualified for the various state elections. On the last day of qualifying, NWAC leadership realized that they were short one candidate. They had no one for the State Board of Elementary and Secondary Education (BESE) 2nd Congressional District-Orleans Parish. "They did however have Keith, a high school drop-out who seldom wore shoes, did not know the difference between the words physical and fiscal, and had no idea where the BESE meetings were held. He had the letters F-U-C-K tattooed across four fingers and legible when he made a fist," Dan said.

"This is how they work, Andre." Each candidate seeking the Ninth Ward Action Committee endorsement was required to pay a "pro-rata" share of expenses. Dan explained the process, "The organization decided how much it would spend for each election. Those expenses were divided among 'endorsed candidates' and candidates running for larger offices paid more, as determined by a secret formula. The group always charged each candidate a little extra "lagniappe" for their troubles." This "little something extra" eventually was enough for one NWAC founder to build a 5,000 square feet home in Eastover with an indoor basketball court. According to IRS records, he never earned more than $21,000. "I guess he knew how to stretch a dollar," Dan said.

NWAC also used the excess cash to build a massive political war chest for the benefit of members like Keith. "This is how a high school dropout becomes President of Louisiana's most important education board," Dan said. Keith ran against a Jesuit Brother who was also an instructor at Loyola University and had served eight years on BESE with an outstanding record of accomplishment. However, NWAC and Keith won a landslide victory with nearly 65% of the vote.

"On Election Day NWAC buses drove to selected areas of town picking up voters for free rides to the polls. Each voter received a two-piece Popeye's fried chicken dinner for the ride home, compliments of the NWAC ticket. NWAC workers organized political parades, stationed 'poll watches' at important locations, operated Election Day phone banks and brought senior citizens from area nursing homes to make groceries after voting," Dan said.

"Is that legal?" I asked.

He tilted his head down and glared at me over the tops of his glasses. "You're kidding, right?" After the BESE victory, NWAC rewarded Keith by setting him up as Assistant Director of the New Orleans Department of Safety and Permits, where he would become wealthy double dipping on two public payrolls. When I met Keith he was planning a European vacation and his mother was driving a Lotus sports car. I wanted some of the trappings of success too.

16

"VO-TECH DIRECTORS WERE A powerful political force in their own right and regulated by BESE. As public employees their political activity was limited by Federal and State campaign finance laws, however, they found ways around that restriction," Dan said. The Directors formed their own political action committee and organized "legal" fund raisers, hired lobbyists, and produced political advertising. The PAC said they held a fund raiser at a Baton Rouge hotel for Keith. "One hundred tickets were sold at $500 each; Keith made an appearance so he could collect the $50,000 legally. The event was actually in a regular hotel room with the PAC director and a six pack of beer," there was nothing about the event that Dan did not know.

Keith had a beer, collected the check, and thanked the organization for their support. He gave his standard political speech to satisfy legal criteria. "How was that?" he asked the director after another beer. "It was a good speech, real good, but if I was a rancher and went out to feed my cattle and only one showed up, I wouldn't feed him the whole load." The $50,000 was reported on Keith's Campaign Finance Report as event proceeds.

BESE also licensed private trade schools, "Proprietary". These are the private trucking schools, welding schools, beauty colleges, court reporting schools, and bartending institutes that advertise on late night television. "They were easy targets for political shake downs because any BESE member could hold up a license request or revoke an existing license. A call for special Proprietary School hearings or investigations would result in thousands of dollars of new campaign contributions," Dan explained.

"In many cases the schools were their own worst enemies. Some provided suspect job training and left unemployable students with large loans to repay. One New Orleans school was closed for financial reasons and the director was instructed to send all teachers and students home and close the building immediately." Dan was shuffling papers around searching for the school's name. "So, how does the director accomplish this without confrontation? He walked out of his office into the hallway and pulled the fire alarm. He waited until everyone was out then locked and chained the front doors. He left through a back door and drove home," Dan said.

17

KEITH WAS A FAST LEARNER in his position at Safety and Permits. Dan explained how this shake down routine worked. "During a dinner meeting at Commander's Palace with real estate developers Keith placed a new hundred dollar bill on the table. "In New Orleans we have high humidity. This can cause construction problems and costly delays. It affects the cement," Keith explained as he rolled the bill in his fingers and shaped it into a small cone. "We use a cone like device, similar to this, but larger. We pour your wet cement into this cone, turn it over and remove the cone." He unrolled the bill and placed it flat on the table.

"If your cement falls over then the humidity has adversely affected the water content balance and we will need to stop your project. Maybe tear it down, in the interest of safety, of course." Keith stroked and caressed the bill like a lover. "Vibrations from a passing streetcar could cause your cement to fall or if the inspector removes the cone too soon. This is not an exact science unfortunately. Don't worry; many NWAC members are skilled in the building trades." The developers got the message and decided to scrap the project," Dan said. He knew all this because he represented the developers once they realized how badly they needed a Louisiana lawyer. "I sure would like to get even with Mr. Keith Hayes," Dan said looking in my direction, smiling.

Keith won the BESE position because of strong well organized political backing. Something Dan assumed I would have as the endorsed Republican candidate. Nevertheless, I felt more comfortable running for New Orleans City Council. I did not have the credentials to manage a state-wide school system with over 800,000 students a $2.5 billion dollar budget, numerous Vo-Tech schools, and 66 local school districts. Dan convinced me otherwise. Dan had the facts and data to indicate that I could win and the fact that BESE was not as heavily contested would work to my advantage. "You can sneak in unnoticed and build a strong political base." Dan said in a convincing manner. "If Keith Hayes won, so could you". I went for the bait like a salt water catfish.

18

HITTING THE CAMPAIGN TRAIL WAS tough, but nobody worked harder or learned faster. The summer weather in South Louisiana is an exhausting combination of stifling heat and humidity. Driving from New Orleans to Baton Rouge under these conditions without air conditioning is almost unbearable. When I purchased my car, I saved $750.00 by buying a model without air conditioning. At that price, it was the only way I could qualify for financing. I kept my tie on because tying it correctly in the first place was a challenge and I was not sure if I could do it again. I had cut the skinny back piece off with scissors because after many attempts I could not get the length correct. When I reached the Capital the knot on the dollar store tie was soaked with perspiration, and had bled red and blue die onto my white shirt that created an interesting and not often seen rainbow effect around my neck. The back of my shirt stuck to the cheap plastic seat covers and my pants and underwear were soaked.

Qualifying for state office lasts only three days, Tuesday - Thursday and was held in the Secretary of State's office in the capital building. I arrived on Wednesday with a personal check for $400. I was not aware that there was an additional $250 dollar charge due as a political party fee. The Democrat and Republican state organizations each received funds from this fee. I did not have another $250 in my checking account and the Secretary of State would not accept personal checks anyhow but I felt encouraged because no one else qualified for the BESE seat, as Dan predicted. I planned to return the next morning with the additional $250.

On Thursday morning, I was eager to get an early start in an effort to avoid the heat, but the temperature was already 90 degrees by 7:30AM. Whitney Bank redeemed $650 of US savings bonds that represented the majority of my financial assets. The bank lines were long and slow moving and interstate traffic was still backed up due to continuing construction. Construction crews placed cement barriers to separate oncoming traffic. These barriers unintentionally created a solid wall for miles. Critters were unable to cross, became confused, and added to mile after mile of road kill. The heat and stench in the slow moving traffic with windows down smelled like a slaughter house. I arrived at the Secretary's office with only one hour to spare and again soaking wet, overheated, and disheveled. When qualifying time is up, it's up! There are no exceptions. The next opportunity would be in four years.

I handed over my cash and began filling out the necessary paperwork. The office walls were lined with poster boards handwritten in marker across the top of each was the name of each specific office. The qualified candidates were listed below in the order in which they qualified. On the far side of the room the listings for the BESE districts were posted. "Oh God", three others were now qualified for my race. Two were Democrats and one a Republican, Dr. Larry Scott, Jasper Juneau and Dr. Craig Demerast, Delgado's President. "Could I see the paperwork for the BESE candidates?" I asked in a dejected tone. "That is not allowed until all qualifying has closed, I'm very sorry!" was the reply. I had only ten minutes to withdraw my qualification and still get my money back. Secretary of State, Keithen walked over and sat next to me. "Son, I have seen you come back and forth for two days. You look like hell, smell, and seem confused. You should not be here. But you are. When I was your age all I wanted was to get laid". As I raised my head from my hands he looked at me eye to eye. "Son, stay in the race. You are one tenacious little SOB. I like you."

19

DR. LARRY SCOTT WAS A former President of the Louisiana Association of Educators (LAE). He had served as a teacher and principal in the St. Tammany Parish School District. Jasper Juneau was a Republican who had run unsuccessfully many times, but believed the party owed him something. Dr. Demerast, a Democrat, was President of Delgado Community College and counted many state politicians as his friends. I remember meeting him at Delgado back when I registered as a part-time student.

Under Dr. Demarest's leadership, Delgado College had evolved from a trade school into a modern successful community college offering many sought after and profitable career paths. The Delgado School of Allied Health and the Delgado Charity School of Nursing became important components of the New Orleans medical community. The Automobile Technician Program was one of the few in Louisiana to be recognized for outstanding quality by General Motors. Most technicians working at area GM dealerships were trained here.

I learned that not all was peaches and crème at Delgado. Dr. Demerast had a well known weakness for womanizing. He jointly purchased a Chris Craft deep sea fishing boat with a close friend. They intended to take it out on weekends or whenever possible. Demerast routinely canceled blaming his difficult work schedule, but unselfishly encouraged the friend to enjoy the fishing without him.

But, Demerast also told his wife he would be fishing all weekend and would be unreachable. He could then spend Saturday and Sunday at the friend's house screwing his friend's wife. He had an arrangement with the harbor master, if the Chris-Craft happened to return early, Demerast received ample warning.

Demerast had been pursuing a recently hired young redhead art instructor at the college; she finally agreed to a "fishing trip". At about 50 miles out, they cut the engine, began drinking and were soon screwing on the aft deck. This area of the Gulf was patrolled by F-14s from Bellchase Naval Air Station performing drug intervention and training missions. A young pilot flew over the Chris-Craft for an inspection flyover, noticed what was going on, and radioed the others. Soon fighter jets were circling like a swarm of hornets. The redhead, while bent over the railing with her swimsuit bottom around one ankle looked up and waived to the pilots. Demerast smiled and gave them the finger.

Delgado's 501(c)3 Foundation has been accused of numerous financial misadventures. Proceeds from the annual Las Vegas night scholarship fundraiser were used to purchase a Cadillac for Dr. Demarest's personal use. He signed questionable sole source contracts with state politicians and their friends leading to audit exceptions. The Delgado bus was rented out for profit and was seen on Bourbon Street transporting drunken Japanese businessmen at 2AM. A Metairie computer company, Gulf Systems Co., gave the Demerast BESE campaign $27,000. Delgado College paid Gulf Systems $830,000 in two years for computer services of questionable value. Craig Demerast insisted the, "contribution had nothing to do with the companies' contracts."

Dr. Demerast's hiring practices promoting nepotism and political patronage at the college had raised eyebrows. Delgado employed two Jefferson Parish School Board members, a local constable, a member of the Board of Trustees of State Colleges and Universities and the Trustee's sister, the daughter and niece of another Board of Trustees member, the Daughter of the Louisiana University System President, and the brother of State Senate President from Chalmette. Colleen Delaney was in her early 20's and served as a student representative on the Board of Trustees. Demerast hired her as his personal assistant. He promoted her to Coordinator of the Slidell and Covington campuses. She had only an Associate degree, but supervised faculty with masters and PHD degrees. Delgado faculty had not had a raise in years but Demerast raised Delaney's pay annually. Demerast also promoted his secretary, Nora Napoli, to executive assistant with a 20% pay raise.

The State of Louisiana named a committee to investigate possible violations of the State's ethic codes at Delgado College. The results were presented to the State Ethics Commission for a ruling. No violations were found because no public officials supervised their immediate family members. "Everyone has got to work some place," Dr. Demerast said.

Jasper Juneau, the other BESE candidate, lived in Jefferson Parish and worked on issues affecting education for decades. He was a fixture at local school board meetings for years and was trusted by local Superintendents and school board members alike. He had also spent years working for Republican causes and candidates. At this time, he was over 70 years old, but would most likely win the official Republican endorsement. These guys were no better than me and I was not intimidated anymore.

20

AT THE CONCLUSION OF ELECTION qualifying the New Orleans paper ran a series of informative articles listing the qualifications, goals, and background information on candidates running in each race. My three opponents listed impressive accomplishments, numerous degrees, and unique experiences. They described in detail the issues they planned to tackle as a member of BESE. High School graduation requirements, drop-out rates, teacher evaluations, high school exit exams, and Minimum Foundation spending reform was discussed in great detail. The articles ran at least one full column with a professional black and white photo. I did not have the necessary photo. "Not a big deal. Come by the office and our photographer will snap a picture," the reporter said with a tone of voice indicating annoyance. My article ran only about three inches long with a photo that resembled a post office mug shot. My political career seemed dead in the water.

The calls from political hacks, campaign managers, and glad flies started immediately after qualifying closed. They all claimed to have been responsible for great victories and memorable campaigns, for a fee they could guarantee my victory. One Political and Governmental Relations outfit claimed that they could deliver the Republican nomination. On the initial call, they dropped names like cheerleaders drop boyfriends. The Pontchartrain Hotel was on St. Charles Avenue along the original streetcar line and was a favorite stop for uptown lawyers and business people heading to the Central Business District from the Garden and the University Districts. The Hotel valued tradition and had been an important part of the New Orleans social scene for decades. Hotel personnel decided in this bastion of tradition rearrange the hotel restaurant and moved a grand piano only an inch a day in order to keep the regular patrons from noticing any change. This is where I believed politicians were supposed to have meetings.

The two representatives of St. Clayman and Associates made outlandish promises no one could guarantee. "We have studied your race. You should get 65% of the vote," they said. "Tell me about my opponents. How could I win so easily?" They could not name the other candidates and the contract they produced was a standard fill-in-the-blanks type, except that they had used the same document before. The name of another candidate was erased and my name written in blue ball point. The proposed fee for their services was $50,000 and all other campaign expenses were an additional charge. I thanked Frick and Frat for their time and got the hell out. The business of politics draws a lot of bloodsucking parasites and I was lucky recognize these interlopers.

21

THE REPUBLICAN PARTY OF JEFFERSON Parish sponsored the first Candidates Forum. The "official" party endorsement would be decided here. This represented the Republican version of the Good Housekeeping Seal of Approval. The loser was expected to withdraw and support the "Official Republican." This year, there was an especially large crop of local Republican candidates since the National Republican Party was expected to keep the White House. These newbie's appeared to be lawyers of mediocre accomplishments, questionable ability, and weak credentials wresting for Federal appointments, judgeships, and contracts expected to come this way. The room was full of campaign workers walking up and down the aisles carrying their candidate's signs and shaking hands. They wore political buttons and American flag stickers that were given out at the door.

As one of the smaller elections, the BESE forum was the last of the evening allowing me time to move around the arena, solicit support, see old friends, and make new ones. "Allen, I know you helped me. But I am committed to Jasper. I have known him for years," said Robert Warner as he paused briefly from back slapping and glad handing. The College Republican's push poll was run on his behalf. Now it was a struggle for him to remember my name.

"It's Andre, not Allen!" I said.

"I wish you had talked to me sooner," he said as he looked at his watch.

"Don't make excuses and besides, how many polls did Jasper run for you? I helped you and now you can't support me on one vote." I said out of disappointment not anger.

"I won't support you because you cannot win. You have no chance. I can't burn political capital for a kid. Go home and make it easy for everybody. Besides Jasper already has the vote locked up," he said.

"There was a time when you were in these shoes. I stood with you! Remember?" Evidently his memory was selective.

"This is different. You don't understand," he said while turning away.

Each candidate was allowed five minutes to deliver a speech and then a fifteen minute question and answer period followed. Jasper talked about his plans for reform and seemed to have the attitude that the party owed this to him. His presentation was poor and his speaking style was stuttering and difficult reminding me of fingernails on a chalkboard. Much of his time was spent recounting his experience as a motorcycle police officer in 1958 when he escorted the Eisenhower motorcade around New Orleans. His five minutes extended to twenty and he received a standing ovation. His question and answer session was a love fest.

A search of public records uncovered a proposed contract between the Louisiana Department of Education and the Peoples Republic of China for the purchase of pencils. The contract had been submitted to the State Auditor for review where it was secretly copied and passed on to me. This was the first such contract ever proposed between China and the Louisiana Dept of Education and expected to be controversial.

"How can we teach our children to love Democracy, fight for freedom and support our free enterprise system while they are writing with communist pencils? Pencils that should be supplied by American workers supporting American families! What is the lesson we are teaching our children?" I asked from the podium. "Listen my children and you shall hear of the midnight ride of Paul Revere, the Chinese are coming, the Chinese are coming! Where does my opponent stand on this most important matter? His silence speaks volumes! As patriotic Republicans, we must demand answers! If Mr. Jasper Juneau supports Communism abroad, then he is probably a member of the ACLU at home!"

If Jasper and the ACLU support pencils from Chairman Mao in math classrooms today, then they will certainly support the Communist Manifesto in history classrooms tomorrow. What would Ike think?" Many in attendance nodded in agreement and looked over at Jasper in a menacing way. A small group of old veterans stood up placed their right hands over their hearts and began reciting the Pledge of Allegiance.

Over the commotion Jasper was heard yelling. "That is absurd! I will not stand for this outrage!" he said in a pitch higher than usual. "I have never seen such a contract. We buy nothing from Red China! I am not a member of the ACLU! I shook President Eisenhower's hand for God's sake!"

It sure was easy to rattle his cage. Copies of the document were passed out on cue with Chinese Government signatures and official red stamps.

The votes were taken and I drove home awaiting the results. The phone was ringing as I opened the door. "Jasper won by a very small percentage. You did extremely well. Much better than anyone expected." The party chairman said in a fatherly tone. "You should also know that Robert Warner took the floor and fought hard on your behalf. In private he said that you were going to peal the bark off of that old fool Jasper and he said you two are now even." I was surprised.

"Mr. Chairman," I asked. "If I violate rules and run as an unendorsed Republican, will the party forgive me?" He was quiet for a long minute. "If you win, you will be forgiven immediately!" Bingo!

22

DAN WAS EAGER TO HELP me "learn the ropes" about campaign financing schemes. "Andre, this is Dan. How are you doing, buddy?" he said in a cheerful tone. "When can you get down here? We have something for you."

I arrived at his French Quarter office and was greeted with a friendly hug. "We read the article in the paper and see that those tight ass reporters don't like you, but we do and that's all that matters!" Dan motioned to his beautiful assistant Camille. "You ever get tired of that political foolishness? Maybe you should try to earn an honest living for once" The maximum allowable contribution amount in a BESE race from any single source was $1,000.00. Dan handed me an envelope containing $20,000.00. "Don't worry!" he said. "That money does not violate campaign finance reporting requirements." He explained that the money was from twenty different people and therefore legal. Dan provided each individual name in order for me to complete the State Financial Reports correctly. He reminded me that he is a lawyer.

"OK" I said. It seemed logical.

"Call if you need anything," he said as I drove off.

The first place I spent some of Dan's campaign funds was at Tulane University. The University's book store offered many titles on important educational, policy, governance, and reform issues. I bought them all and planned to read them all. "Those are some interesting titles you have there. I'm Louis Barrilleaux, Dean of the College of Education," he said as he extended his hand. "I don't think we have met."

I explained that I was a candidate for BESE and he offered to help any time. He looked through the books in my hand and suggested others. During the conversation, I learned that towards the end of the 1968 football season Tulane's head coach resigned. Dr. Louis Barrilleaux finished the season as head coach. He had a ball signed by the team in his office. I promised to call soon, as he insisted.

I loved visiting Tulane University campus. Each building is alive with memories, enshrined in worn stairs and plastered walls, and in initials carved in door frames by forgotten lovers, reminders that time eventually will take everything. In these buildings, we are always mindful of the passing of generations, each must yield to the next, including our own. I loved visiting the campus, but, to me, a Tulane education was only a pipe dream for the son of a former campus maintenance electrician. Most Tulane students were from wealthy East Coast families, many from Long Island, New York. My family came from Rabbit Island, mostly marshland and accessible only by the L&N railroad or by boat, in Lake Saint Catherine near the Rigolets and Chef Menteur Pass, and the 9th Ward.

After I purchased the books, I used additional funds to print political material including yard signs and push cards. At my father's insistence, I ordered the campaign yard signs from a union printer; Democrats always looked for the "union bug" on printed political material. A Union Bug is a small circular logo indicating the AFL-CIO printing. Republicans were indifferent to this special insignia, since Louisiana was a Right to Work state.

23

LIKE A LIGHTING STRIKE, PAUL Tanner unexpectedly entered my life and became an important influence in both my political and personal life. "Mr. Dupree, this is Terri DiMarco. I am personal assistant to Mr. Tanner, he has asked me to call," she said in a no nonsense professional tone.

Mr. Tanner was the richest person in Louisiana, by his own admission and according to Fortune Magazine, he was number 134 of the wealthiest people in America, operating Louisiana's largest independent oil and gas production company called 'Tanner Energy.' He was active in nearly every political race and usually gave generous contributions. Mr. Tanner was also the point man for the 1988 National Republican Convention in New Orleans. Fund raising, site selection, special events and platform development was his responsibility.

Mr. Tanner first hit the national spotlight with his suggestion to former Secretary of the Interior Donald Hodel that the federal government could raise funds by selling off Federal lands and parks. Secretary Hodel gave serious consideration to the suggestion causing a whirlwind of national outrage. Time magazine ran a cover with a silver shoe, "cabinet secretary places foot in mouth." Mr. Tanner was born poor in east Texas. He entered the prestigious Kinkaid School in Houston on scholarship and later enrolled at LSU because it had a strong petroleum engineering program and was comparatively inexpensive. He heard that all a freshman LSU student needed to bring on the first day was a toothbrush.

"Mr. Tanner would like to see you in his office tomorrow at 2:30 pm." Ms. DiMarco said.

The room adjacent to Mr. Tanner's office was used as a waiting area for appointments. The walls were covered in a dark mahogany paneling and had glove soft ox blood leather chairs. Western sculptures by Frederic Remington lined the walls along with a series of oil painted portraits of the heroes of the Alamo hanging on one wall. Pictures of various oil production platforms and oil wells lined the other. On the far side of the room was a brass engraved panel with an abbreviated version of a Robert Frost poem.

> The woods are lonely dark and deep.
> But I have promises to keep.
> And miles to go before I sleep.

My wait ended abruptly with the entrance of two men in dark suits. They looked at me, looked around the room and said nothing as they stood with their hands behind their backs near the right side of the door, keeping their eyes trained on me. Mr. Tanner was moving very fast and had little time. "It is nice to meet you. I hear you screwed and barbecued our candidate, Jasper, the other night at the endorsement forum," he said. "Don't worry! I love competition! Here is a contribution to help your campaign. You make the runoff and there will be more. Go get'em, Tiger." He left with the two bodyguards.

24

WHILE I FACED TOUGH OPPONENTS skilled with political savvy and connections, they faced a 'street smart' kid from the 9th Ward. Louisiana has an open primary system. All candidates run together regardless of party affiliation and registered voters can vote for any candidate on the ballot. I believed the BESE race would be decided in the primary since the leading Republican would most likely win the runoff, because the 1st BESE District was majority Republican. The Democrat in the runoff would simply not have enough support to overcome the Republican advantage in numbers of voters. If I could beat Jasper in the primary, then I could be the next BESE member from this District. I had to beat Jasper. Sounded easy enough!

Posing as Jasper supporters, a small group of former College Republican friends went to his campaign headquarters and offered to help in any way possible. They spent two days stuffing envelops answering the phone and earning trust. With the help of Republican headquarters, the Jasper campaign had developed a long list of residences that requested a campaign sign for their front yards. Many people requested political signs because the 1x2x4 wooden stakes were perfect for growing Creole tomatoes. The College Republican sign team loaded an old pickup truck and headed out to destroy Jasper's campaign. Jasper thanked them over and over for their help while he pitched in to help load their truck.

A hard-luck section of Jefferson Highway was home to many cheap hotels that rented rooms by the hour. Drug deals were common as was crime, violence, and prostitution. The Jefferson Parish Sheriff tried unsuccessfully for years to close these businesses and clean up the area, "The armpit of Jefferson Parish." Many white collar Jefferson Parish residents that worked in New Orleans took this route home since they headed to the suburbs avoiding interstate traffic. They were surprised to see that Jasper had such strong support here as his signs lined the roadway for miles.

Next the crew started working their way down Jasper's location list. Most houses in New Orleans are constructed of wood. Rather than using the tomato sticks for yard signs as instructed these signs were nailed directly onto the sides of houses. In St. Tammany Parish live oaks are treated with a reverence usually reserved for religious icons. The crew nailed "Jasper for BESE" signs directly to oaks. Some trees received two or three signs to assure visibility from all angles. Most were placed high so that removal was difficult. The "turncoat" crew then dropped off the remaining tomato sticks and Republican location list at my home and dumped the remaining Jasper signs in a trash bin. I suspected this kind of skullduggery, but did not acknowledge or condone the activity that way I could always deny any involvement.

The calls started around 5:00 PM as people returned home to find "Jasper for BESE" signs nailed into their walls. Hunks of wood were removed with the nails as they were the type designed to resist easy extraction. Jasper was relaxed and alone in his office wondering why his sign team had not yet returned. Then the calls started, the most unsettling came from a local television station seeking comment on the developing St. Tammany live oak controversy. Jasper was fined $75 for each sign nailed to a tree as a littering charge and he faced significant charges for sign removal. Additionally, he received a court date for each individual litter citation. He looked foolish and seemed unbelievable with only first names and no other information on these mysterious "boys." "They were such nice boys. So eager to help and so interested in politics. I don't understand," Jasper said to the reporters as he promised to repair all damage. Repairing the destruction to his campaign would prove more difficult. I waited two days before calling the names on Jasper's sign list. Most were now eager to do anything to help defeat that "moron," as they called him. I began placing my campaign signs throughout the district using Jasper's tomato sticks and calling on his location contacts. He never knew what hit him!

25

MORE POLITICAL SKULLDUGGERY LAY AHEAD.
Two competitive Republicans candidates fighting it out created a unique opportunity for the Democratic Party to sneak in and steal an unlikely victory. For their strategy to work they had to make sure both Republicans were strong enough to attract significant support, thus splitting the Republican vote between each candidate. I received an invitation from the endorsement committee of the Regular Democratic Association (RDA). This is the oldest continuously operating political organization in the city. The members smoke cigars and drive big Cadillacs. Most are from the Irish Channel or Mid-city area and grew up working the warehouses and docks lining the Mississippi River.

The meeting was held at the Lakeview home of an Orleans Parish Judge who also happened to be an RDA member who "made good." Dr. Demerast spent time in quiet private discussions with various RDA members, Jasper stood off in the corner alone, I moved around trying to meet as many new faces as possible. Dr. Demerast spoke first. "Louisiana does not have a Community College system. We have only three community colleges in the entire state," he said. "Why do you think Louisiana universities offer expensive remedial math and English programs for incoming freshman?" he answered his own question. "Because we do not have a proper system to handle students that are not ready for college level work." He pounded the table top to make the point. "Did you know that universities are paid

1/3 more per credit hour taught in remedial courses than regular undergrad work?" The RDA members looked surprised. "Since we do not have a community college system they enter the four year university system directly as the only alternative. This makes remedial classes a necessity and it also makes open admissions necessary! That places our universities at a competitive disadvantage."

He had more. "BESE controls the Louisiana Vocational Technical System. There are eight regional Vo-Tech campuses located around the state that should be converted to community colleges. Nevertheless, BESE is reluctant to make this important change because community colleges are controlled by a different board, The Board of Trustees for Colleges and Universities. BESE will not make this change, I will. Give me your vote!"

After the applause, Dr. Demarest walked directly over and placed his arm around my shoulders. "Hang in there Andre! My people say you are going to be the one to beat!" Before I could answer, he was off in a corner with the RDA President Frank Bradley, speaking in whispers and looking in my direction. Frank would become my nemesis.

Frankly, I was intimidated by his presentation, but not afraid to attack. "My credentials do not measure up against Dr. Demerast. We all know this. What you don't know is what I have in common with many of you. My grandfather operated a dry cleaning business on North Robinson Street for thirty five years. My other grandfather handled baggage at the Union Passenger Terminal until they stopped the passenger trains. He got through the Depression by rebuilding flat head Ford V-8's at Bohn Ford." RDA guys were pipe fitters, brick layers, and boiler makers. "I started delivering the *States-Item* evening paper at twelve years of age and have not been unemployed since. I worked as a dishwasher and bus boy at West End restaurants. I cleaned the dining room and the bathrooms and usually worked two jobs through high school and college. My father is a union electrician with IBEW Local 130 and was maintenance guy at Tulane. I am not a College President, but neither are any of you. All I want is fair consideration."

"The Republicans have not officially endorsed me and I don't have very much campaign money. Most think I have no chance. But like many of you, I have always been the underdog, my back has always been against the wall. I'll give it a hell of a fight! Please do what you can on my behalf." As I was stepping down, I reached over to shake the hand of an older RDA member who was in my path. He grabbed my hand and turned it so that he could study it closely. He noticed the small circular scars on the top of my hand just above the knuckles. As teenagers we proved our toughness by holding lit cigarettes against our hands until the flesh burned. The old man turned his own hand to reveal similar but much older scars. He placed both his hands on my shoulders and kissed each cheek, a greeting usually reserved for family.

26

THE NEXT MORNING I KEPT a lunch meeting with Frank, the RDA President, and drove to his Metairie office as planned. His face retained the marks of heavy adolescent acne and his small chin, narrow jaw, and over bite bore a resemblance to a Sheephead fish. The RDA had not yet announced their endorsement decisions and I assumed he would have the results. One wall of his RDA/Law office was covered by an oversized American flag. "What is this? It feels familiar." I asked while fondling a jelly filled clear packet to the right of his desk clock. Frank was a Plaintiff Attorney and had been involved in many high profile cases. "A breast implant," he said.

His assistant interrupted with an important incoming call. She was middle age, attractive and married to the RDA's Vice President and Frank's old friend, David Levet. Frank hired her as a favor to David when their family was experiencing difficult financial times. "She never wears panties under her skirt. At first, it was a job requirement. Now, she likes it," he said laughing. "When she comes back here ask her to raise her skirt and show you. She loves to show off," he continued. "You should ask Congressman Lynchard. The last time he was here we tag teamed her for three hours. It is becoming a habit with that SOB. Every time he is in New Orleans he wants to visit and discuss "drilling issues." Her favorite position is bent over the copy machine with one leg raised on a stool and her skirt pulled up." Frank said the Congressman taught her that position. Something he learned in D.C. "The Congressman is inline to become Speaker of the House if a few things fall his way," Frank said. "We must treat him nice". I knew Congressman Lynchard only from his campaign commercials which promoted, "Christian upbringing and family values." His three children and pretty young wife were always campaigning at his side.

"Doreen, will you come in here and raise your skirt for Andre?" Frank asked over the intercom system. "Just answer the phone" was her reply.

"I was promised that contract. I did my part, now I expect the work. The trucks have been purchased and I hired the drivers," Frank said to the other party on the phone. Frank owned a trucking company called AFMTC (American Freight and Motor Trucking Company) and was promised a lucrative contract hauling produce from Oakland, California to Green Bay, Wisconsin in exchange for legal work that he recently completed. American Freight and Motor Trucking Company was actually Another Fucking Minority Trucking Company (AFMTC) indicating the fraudulent minority ownership Frank established.

"Andre, do you have time for lunch? I know a great place across the lake" Frank asked. The restaurant was a short drive to the causeway from his office and then a twenty four mile straight shot across Lake Pontchartrain to Mandeville. "Sure, why not," I said. I had nothing else planned and wanted to use the time to get to know him better. Frank was considering the purchase of a Mercedes sedan, a late model recent trade-in and appeared to be in outstanding condition. "I want to test drive it across the lake and back. If it has no problems, then I will sign the papers later today," he told the salesman.

Frank drove through the toll booth, handed the attendant a dollar and pushed the accelerator to the floor. The 500SD was capable of reaching 185MPH. The guard rail appeared to be a solid concrete wall and the white lane markers blurred together as Frank pushed the Mercedes to its limit. We passed cars traveling at 65MPH like they were slow Model T's. Our closing speed with the other traffic was 120MPH leaving no room for error. "Where are the cup holders in this damn car?" He asked as he looked in all possible locations for the nonexistent cup holders. "Fucking Germans!" We swerved from lane to lane until, to my great relief, he gave up looking for holders and refocused his attention back on the road.

"In the old days" he said. "The activities of the RDA, Old Regulars, they were called back then, were run by the Choctaw Club." Frank was proud of the RDA history and viewed himself as the heir apparent. "Mayor Martin Behrman was the first great Old Regular mayor. He made New Orleans a modern city. But Robert Maestri, another great, saved the city from bankruptcy. In 1942, he was reelected without campaigning," Frank said. "Then that pussy, de Lesseps "Chep" Morrison, ruined everything. How could a 33 year old from the town of New Roads beat Maestri? Nevertheless, you still see many people entering the polls on Election Day carrying their pink RDA ballots." He was right. I remember my grandfather studying the pink ballot and thumb tacking it to the door jam in the kitchen. "Why pink?" I wondered. "All RDA literature was printed on pink paper to resemble the coloration of Confederate money. It's not because we are courting the Gay Pride vote as some nickel dick reporters have speculated over the years."

The causeway is two separate bridges with two lanes each heading north and south. We passed two cars side by side using the emergency lane, leaving only inches between my side of the car and the guard rail. "I hope the brakes work as well as everything else on this car," I said as we reached the north side toll plaza.

We arrived at "The Po-Boy Tavern," a popular place that specialized in local dishes. I did not mind Frank eating off my plate; I did mind the disgusting throat clearing noise he made before spitting into his napkin, balling it up, and setting it on the table. He ordered a Dr. Pepper with half ice and two lime wedges and an oyster po-boy dressed and onion rings. "Dressed" po-boys is the typical New Orleans way of ordering, meaning everything comes with the sandwich – lettuce, tomato, pickles, mayonnaise. The part of my stomach still intact after the "test drive" was completely lost looking at the balled up napkin. I could see the cook through an opening used to pass the orders from the kitchen. She was overweight, sweating, wearing a yellowed and stained tee shirt tank top and swearing at the other kitchen help. She did not shave under her arms and looked overwhelmed. Frank's onion rings were placed on a plate and then the French bread was measured according to groove marks cut into the counter top. Short of hands the frustrated cook used her armpit to hold Frank's bread while she sliced tomatoes and readied other items.

"Here is the deal," he said in a way that indicated play time was over. "Andre, you have the RDA endorsement. We feel that you can beat that other Republican fool, Jasper. "With our help and assistance from some additional friends, your place in the runoff is assured. Unfortunately for you, people will then begin paying attention and will realize that you are only 23 years old. Dr. Demerast's credentials will carry the day and you will certainly lose." He devoured the po-boy and chewed and spoke at the same time. He found a small curly black hair on the sandwich, studied it momentarily between his thumb and index finger, flicked it onto the floor and continued eating and talking. "However, you could drop out of the runoff quickly and save everyone a lot of expense and trouble. In which case, the current Register of Conveyances in City Hall will immediately resign and you will be named to fill the unexpired vacated term."

"What does the Register of Conveyances do and where is his office?" I asked.

"Every important legal document related to the sale of property and other legal contracts in Orleans Parish are recorded in that office. It is located in the basement of Civil District Court building next to City Hall," Frank said.

"I have never heard of that office. Why would I want to work in a basement? It sounds like political Siberia and I am not Ivan Denisovich." I said thinking out loud.

"Who the fuck is Ivan whatever, is he from Chalmette? It doesn't matter. I have an envelope for you. It is the best way for the RDA to express our appreciation for your cooperation and acceptance of this outstanding offer. Do with it as you wish." Frank asked for Dupree campaign bumper stickers and flyers. "If anyone starts sniffing around about that contribution, just say we were buying Dupree political material."

I could see the stack of bills inside but did not pick up the envelope that he slid to the center of the table.

The Conveyance office was important for another reason. It was the only city office with non-classified employees. The thirty employees were political, not civil service. "For these reasons the Register's office may be the most important of all for a young elected official. Think of the possibilities," Frank said.

"What if I make the runoff and stay in to win." I asked.

"You can't win. Winning is not possible. Make the most of this opportunity. You stay and lose, you get nothing. Don't be stupid, you will lose."

I excused myself from the table, but did not notice Frank following close behind. Standing in front of the urinal I was startled when he reached around and began fiddling with my pants. "What the hell are you doing?" I did not know that these secretive type discussions are usually settled in the bathrooms of public places. Privacy is assured. Surveillance is unlikely and others can be easily kept out. Frank was trying to place the envelope in my pants pocket and assumed that my trip to the bathroom was an indication of offer acceptance. I was concerned about the status of his mental health, but I needed the cash for the campaign. The money would come in handy during the runoff, "Mother's Milk", as they say. Funny thing, Frank was not the most bizarre and dysfunctional character I would encounter as I fell deeper into the rabbit hole of Louisiana politics, but he was close to being the most dysfunctional.

27

ONCE I RECEIVED THE RDA endorsement, a number of unsettling and unexpected bad things began to happen right away. The RDA had many enemies, including most business groups and organizations like Louisiana Association of Industry and the Public Affairs Business Council and the Republican Party. Many good government groups like The Alliance for Better State Government considered the RDA to be the foundation of evil in Louisiana politics. As a result, all other Republican candidates began to add Jasper's campaign materials with their own mailings. They held joint press conferences announcing their support for my opponent. Republicans funneled funds, campaign support and volunteers towards Jasper, and used state party funds to print his cards and signs. The effort was no longer to elect Jasper, but becoming a crusade to punish me and defeat the RDA's game plan of using me to elect Dr. Demarest.

Campaigning everyday door to door is hard, but worthwhile. Each day, I selected a different subdivision and did not leave that area until I had knocked on every available door. I left tiny red spots on each door as my knuckles were bleeding from the endless knocking. To look older and more professional I wore one of my new suits recently purchased from the local discount retailer. Two friends followed close by and handed out cards and signs as I shook hands. Occasionally, we were invited inside and were tempted by the cool air conditioning, but refused because time equaled votes. Some voters knew nothing about the Education Board race or my candidacy. "Son, in 1965, I lost everything I had to Betsy," an older man said through his locked screen door. "No sir, I am running for BESE. It is The State Board of Elementary and Secondary Education. I'm not talking about the hurricane!"

Football games and politics go hand and hand as the large crowds are ideal targets for electioneering. The Professional Football Players Association planned their first ever strike as a dispute over pay and free agency rights escalated. A strike was called and teams were forced to fill positions with; wannabees, has-beens, unknowns, and dreamers. The new rosters were not available since the teams were finalized on very short notice. Organized labor took the side of the striking players and called the new players that crossed picket lines "scabs".

"We noticed the union bug logo on your campaign material. Most Republicans would not use a union printer, but then again, your father was IBEW," said the unidentified Teamster Official on the other end of the phone. "We have access to the team rosters including numbers, positions and names for tomorrow's game at the Dome. We thought you could use it, Andre"

I spent the next five hours at the All Night Quick Print making thousands of flyers with the new "scab" roster on one side, my campaign information on the other, the union bug on both and folded long ways. I had a short, restless sleep and awoke eager to see the morning paper. The roster was still unavailable at print time and the paper ran an apology instead. My car was riding low and scraped bottom as we entered the Dome Stadium parking area with a trunk full of flyers and a car full of volunteers. Large signs advertising "Free Scab Rosters" were attached to long tomato sticks so that they could be seen above the crowds.

We set up at several strategic positions around the stadium. Unfortunately, Jasper with a well organized team of "official" Republican volunteers arrived sooner and claimed the best locations. Arriving football fans encountered Jasper's group first as they entered the gates and politely accepted the literature from his eager volunteers. Fans walked further and realized that "Free Scab Rosters" were available. Most discarded the Jasper material and waited in lines to receive the Dupree 'scab' rosters. As game time approached, lines grew longer and less patient. Officers from the NOPD showed up to help move the lines along and maintain order. Litter cans were full and the ground around our feet was carpeted with trashed Jasper material. Radio announcers thanked the Dupree campaign "on air" for providing the roster information. In the stadium, Dupree flyers were passed from seat to seat as fans tried to determine who was playing on the field.

"This is a stupid waste of time" a frustrated Franklin volunteer said as she dumped her remaining flyers in the trash and walked away. Jasper found a cardboard box and was seen searching the ground for reusable flyers. A wasted effort, as most were trampled under foot by eighty thousand football fans. 'Street Smarts' won again.

28

THE RACE WAS STILL VERY tight and I could not leave anything to chance. I called on Dan's expertise. "Dan, this is Andre. Can I come see you? I need help." The election was only two weeks away and I had to generate more attention and more grassroots get out the vote efforts.

"Andre, whatever you need." he said. This would require careful attention to detail and no mistakes. I explained my idea to Dan and related it to the success I had using sex appeal to recruit UNO College Republicans. "I love it, love it. What a great idea! I think it will work better in this District than anywhere else. Those Republican hypocrites are in for quite a treat," Dan said after hearing my idea.

Dan was eager to carry out the plan and offered a well-reasoned defense of his views on sex, power, and politics as proof. "Sex and the desire for reproductive success are the reason for nearly everything we do, including politics. This plan may be good for my business and also raise the curtain on conservative value charades," he said. We spent the afternoon relaxing at a local steak house working out details and then attended a performance of the opera, La Boheme. According to Dan, I needed culture. "A New Orleanian with culture is one of the world's most interesting people. Without it, you're just a y'at," he said.

Y'at, depending on how it is spoken and in what group is either an insult or a "you're one of us" designation. People in New Orleans regularly say, "Where are you at?" However, if you make that question one word, it comes out, "Y'at?" A y'at, as an insult, is an expression of a low-class, uneducated person. I did not want to be seen as a y'at anymore.

The first location I visited was the Mandeville Fine Foods grocery, upscale and expensive. They specialize in wine and take out gourmet meals for busy families and overstressed professionals. Dan's girls, the same girls I generously paroled as a member of the Parish Executive Committee, looked beautiful wearing thin Jackie Kennedy style dresses made of thin material, heals, and no slips. The "girls" stood at the store exits with the sun to their backs and the outlines of their striking figures visible as customers exited the store. The girls carried small purses and wore buttons with the red, white, and blue Republican pachyderm. They spoke like Loyola graduates with friendly smiles. "Please vote for Andre Dupree. He is running for BESE."

The store manager demanded approval from his district level supervisor. "Politics are not allowed on company property. Rule 18, page 16, paragraph 2 of the company management handbook." He recited from memory, but was easily convinced to reconsider his position after a very short closed door meeting with the Dupree campaign workers. He was middle age, overweight and had spent his entire adult life working here at this store. He emerged from the closed door meeting wearing the Dupree for BESE sticker and asked a store clerk to provide water to the hard working ladies. The manager also had a stack of Dupree stickers that he handed out to employees.

The store manager did offer some good advice. "The secret to good fast food is to find out when they change their grease," he said. He explained that the Health Department requires changing the deep fryer oil once a week. "If you come in towards the end of the schedule your food is fried in week old grease. This is when you have most of your food illness issues." He continued, "Everything begins to taste alike. Onion rings, fries, chicken, and fish have all been cooking in the same old grease for a week. Tuesday is best. We change everything on Tuesday morning," he said. I was glad the manager had a few minutes with Dan's girls, he needed it!

"Dear, you look so nice. Of course I will vote for Mr. Andre. My son is 30 years old and never married. He is a very nice young man and has a good job. He went to college for two years." The southern lady said as she held hands and spoke with passion. In a quiet voice she continued, "His father thinks he is gay." Dan's girl replied, "Honey, you send him right over. I would love to meet him." The little lady hurried home in her Lincoln Continental with a small dog on her lap and a new green and white Andre Dupree for BESE bumper sticker across the back.

All locations with Dan's girls went well, even the parks and theaters. At the Old Hickory dirt one-mile oval race track on Highway 22, the race cars all had Dupree stickers on their doors and bumpers. Some drivers had the stickers on their helmets. The Mayor of Covington was leaving the North Shore Shopping Center with his wife and two young children not expecting to see his favorite girl, Cyndi. The one he always requested by name. She handed him the Dupree material and asked for his vote. The Mayor was about to say something. He stopped, looked at his wife and children, looked again at Cyndi and her beautiful smile. "Politics" he said under his breath and walked away holding his wife's hand asking the children something about pizza and ice cream.

29

THE NEW ORLEANS PICAYUNE JOURNAL paper was one of the few major metro papers to still issue election endorsements and I desperately needed their support. Their endorsements were printed front page on Election Day under the heading "Our Recommendations." The paper's decisions were based on face-to-face interviews between the editorial staff and the candidate. In a close race, the endorsement meant the difference between winning and losing. I called Dr. Barrilleaux from Tulane and asked for his help. We spent an entire Sunday afternoon at the Tulane Commons drinking coffee and preparing for the newspaper interview.

Dr. Barrilleaux explained to me the fundamental reasons why educational reform in Louisiana is nearly impossible.

"Andre," he said, "Backwards tax structure, distrust between the races, and a maze of overlapping governing levels are insurmountable roadblocks. Poor educational opportunity leads to crime and chronic underachievement. A city or state with a large underclass can never prosper. Consequently, taxes must remain high to support the basic needs of this portion of the population causing further economic stagnation. New businesses considering relocation to the state will factor the cost of private school tuition as a tax that most are unwilling to pay. For years, Louisiana was able to get by on oil revenues. Now, the future depends on providing adequate educational opportunity for all citizens," Dr. Barrilleaux said as he started on his second coffee.

"What is an example of an insurmountable reform roadblock?" I asked.

"There is an anecdotal example of Louisiana's dysfunctional mentality I like to discuss with freshman students," Dr. Barrilleaux said. "Most states appoint independent boards to develop lists of approved books. Each local school board then makes selections from that list. Orders are placed with the various publishers and the books are promptly delivered using UPS or FedEx. In Louisiana, BESE develops an approved list. The local school boards send their orders to the Louisiana School Book Depository (LSBD). The Depository accumulates and compiles these orders and notifies the publishers. The publishers deliver the orders to LSBD warehouses in the Baton Rouge. State personnel spend the summer sorting individual school district orders. In early August, Depository trucks began crisscrossing the state making textbook deliveries in time for the start of the new school year. I'm not making this up!" he said.

Race is misunderstood in Louisiana with tragic results according to Dr. Barrilleaux. "Louisiana high school exit exams will be opposed by black community leaders. Higher graduation requirements will be opposed by black community leaders. Teacher merit pay and professional evaluations proposals will be opposed by black leadership. Higher admission requirements at public colleges and universities will be opposed. This makes whites very angry," Dr. Barrilleaux said. "During a floor discussion of high school graduation requirements an exasperated white State Senator said that if academic standards are unimportant to the black community than we should issue high school diplomas at the same time we issue birth certificates and save everyone a lot of money and trouble." I could understand that frustration, it seemed to make sense.

"Did black leadership simply not want improvement?" I asked.

"Andre, you have much to learn," the Dean said. "Studies prove that education achievement is a generational issue. If your great grandfather learned a trade working as an apprentice, then perhaps your grandfather learned a skill at a state trade school. Then your father would have reasonable expectations of earning a two-year associate degree at the local community college. After generations of struggle you would have a realistic expectation of earning a four year State University Degree. Even today, a large percentage of incoming freshmen at Louisiana State University are the first in their families to reach that level."

"Why is this a problem for blacks?" I asked.

"Segregation finally ended in the seventies. Before that time, blacks by legal requirement attended separate schools. All Louisiana school districts provided adequate high school facilities for white students while offering nearly nothing past the eighth grade for blacks. The few Louisiana public black high schools that did exist were nothing more than agriculture shop programs. Therefore, black college attendance was impossible," Dr. Barrilleaux said.

"The most significant missed opportunity occurred quite recently," he said. "After WWII, the GI Bill made college accessible to middle class America on a grand scale for the first time. It changed society and created wealth and educational opportunity on an unprecedented scale. Blacks could not take full advantage because colleges and universities were still segregated. While no one can reasonably blame today's college students for these historic problems, black families are playing catch-up because others have a hundred and fifty year head start." The Dean was quiet for a moment while I considered his logic.

"Do you see the problem? Is it any wonder that black leaders are distrustful of any reform plan that makes education less accessible, even those based on "high standards." Higher graduation requirements, admission requirements, and testing requirements are viewed suspiciously as efforts to turn back the clock on educational accessibility. Having only achieved accessibility in very recent times, black leaders will fight to keep it," Dr. Barrilleaux said. "The irony is that most of the traditional Creole, Cajun, and Black and White families all have mixed blood, common in Louisiana. We are all cousins!"

"What about the governing structure? Let's talk about that for a minute," I said.

"What a mess! We know that BESE has eight elected members and three members appointed by the Governor for a total of eleven. The State House and Senate both have Education Committees all elected. The State Superintendent of Education is appointed by BESE. Each of the sixty six local school districts are managed by an elected board and appointed local Superintendent. The Governor also employs a Director of Education. The Board of Supervisors oversees LSU. The Board of Trustees for Colleges and Universities oversees the regional colleges and community colleges and the Board of Regents oversees these higher education boards. All members of these boards are appointed by the Governor. Various nongovernmental organizations (NGOs) like teacher union groups, employ lobbyists on a full time basis." He paused to enjoy his coffee for a moment and catch his breath. "All significant elementary and secondary reform proposals require BESE, Senate, and House approval. Accountability is overlapping at so many levels that assigning blame for failure is impossible."

"What a screwed-up mess," I thought.

I was taking notes, but was beginning to feel overwhelmed.

"Do you need a break?" I wanted to continue. "Reform plans initiated in the Legislature are implemented by BESE and the State Department of Education. But purse string control gives the legislature an effective veto tool over BESE policy. The House has on occasion cut Vo-Tech system funding as a protest against sloppy BESE management."

I asked Dean Barrilleaux to stop for a minute while I reviewed my notes. He took the opportunity to finish his coffee.

"The only exception to the purse string funding rule is the Minimum Foundation Program (MFP). This is the budget by which

Louisiana funds public education on a formula basis statewide. It allocates nearly 1/3 of Louisiana's total annual state budget and covers everything from teacher salaries and textbooks to school buses and pencils," he said. "The Legislature cannot change the formula once BESE submits it. If they reject the formula as submitted then the state reverts to the previous year's formula funding levels. Consequently during difficult financial times other important budget categories are hit harder because the massive MFP is untouchable. Special interest groups know that to be included in the MFP is the closest thing to guaranteed funding possible in any Louisiana political arena," he said. "Get control of the MFP and you could be our next Governor!"

"With so much money on the line, BESE members become very popular very fast or hated." He paused for a moment. "Consequently, BESE is a den of snakes that makes other Louisiana political bodies look like a Boy Scout jamboree. You'll feel like you are in the middle of a pack of hungry pit bulls with a pork chop tied around your neck. If you win the primary and stay in the runoff they will come at you with everything." He would be right.

30

I SPENT THE NEXT FEW days preparing for the *Picayune Journal* interview using the Tulane books, my notes from Dr. Barrilleaux's discussions, and developing my own reform ideas.

The long table sat eight on each side and was made of a Formica material that appeared indestructible. Chrome strips ran along the sides. Numerous burn marks remained where lit cigarettes were forgotten and left dangling over the table's edge. Coffee cups and water glasses were placed on the table top and no one bothered to wipe off the rings. Chairs were a heavy oak construction with most of the finish worn off long ago, but surprisingly comfortable. When I walked in four members of the Editorial staff were already seated at the table's far end.

No one smiled or offered to shake hands. I sat down placed my hands on the table and stared directly at the editors' unsure of the oncoming inquisition. Without identifying themselves the questions began. I think I handled the rapid fire session well and felt confident. I became more relaxed and began to enjoy the intellectual sparing.

"I have answered your questions for thirty minutes. With the remaining time, may I share my ideas?" I began before they had a chance to object. "Many inner-city and poor rural children have no reasonable expectations for ever attending college. Louisiana also has some of the highest dropout rates in the country. I propose a plan to increase university admission requirements and raise academic standards while increasing availability and accessibility for all Louisiana kids. The cost will be minimal," I said.

I had their attention. "In the recent past, a high school education was sufficient and was provided by the state in some fashion. Many of the jobs available at that time to high school graduates offered financial security and longevity. Today, those jobs have been exported to Mexico and China. A university education is not a luxury today; it is a necessity. The state was expected to meet its obligations in terms of education necessity in the past and it is today. Every Louisiana student regardless of family income, who earns a 20 on the ACT, takes two years of foreign language and math, has a 2.5 high school GPA will receive free tuition to any Louisiana pubic university or college." They sat upright and cast interested looks across the table.

"Louisiana universities are spending millions on remedial math and English with limited results. Those funds will now be earmarked for this Tuition Opportunity Program since university remedial courses will soon become less necessary. Families will begin to demand the required courses; local school boards will work hard to get students prepared and students of all races and financial backgrounds will have reasonable expectations of college success. Many will be the first in their families to do so. Destructive behavior will become less likely as students will have brighter futures ahead."

"In addition, I propose using the MFP program to fund necessary course offerings at all high schools in all districts statewide. Leaving no one out even the poorest parishes where foreign language instruction and college prep courses are a scarce luxury." The only sound in the room was of fingers tapping in rhythm on the table to my left. The editor to my right was repeatedly rubbing his chin and looking at the ceiling in deep thought. Nothing was said for a long while. "You will learn of our decision when it's printed. Thank you for your time, Mr. Dupree."

31

FRANK BRADLEY WAS THE FIRST to call early Thursday morning. I let the answer machine pick up his call because I was unprepared to discuss my decision to reject his offer. "Wake up, Andre! It looks like you got the paper's endorsement. We expected that to go to Dr. Demarest. Not a problem. You are going to love the Conveyance office job." For the first time I felt convinced that I could do well in the primary.

I was spending the remaining campaign cash on last minute radio spots to build momentum heading into the runoff and enjoyed reading the paper's endorsement.

> Andree Dupree shows a strong grasp of the
> issues facing this increasingly important board.
> Providing educational opportunity to all
> qualified Louisiana youth, "is the state's best
> chance of improving education." His unique views would
> be helpful on a board that must handle such
> important and complex matters.

I pushed hard towards the finish line the last few days. More campaign signs were placed, radio spots were increased and I continued to knock on doors from sunup to sundown.

A confident Dr. Demarest did nothing out of the ordinary. He had his regular two hour morning breakfast each day and worked out at the Delgado gym in the evening. College business was handled during the day as usual. He did not deviate from his ordinary routine and was as confident as a heavily favored prize fighter. He began calling me the young lad, eager young man, or nice young fellow. In a WWM radio interview, he said that I would make a good adjunct professor, if I ever finished a degree. "I would need some life experience first," he said.

I knew that Frank's deal was about as useless as his pink confederate money. The current Register of Conveyances, Vincent Schiro, is Frank's business partner. Vincent has been a loyal RDA member for decades and all non-classified employees in his office were RDA members. He continues to campaign at this advanced age because late one summer night Pope Pius X appeared from a photo on a wall in Vincent's kitchen sat at the table and advised him to run "again and again." Vincent's wife Mabel will confirm this as the gospel truth.

As business partners, Frank and Vincent formed Holy Hands Construction Company and proceeded to develop a north shore subdivision. Saint Anthony's Acres was planned with Saint Joseph Street, Saint Ann Street, Saint Jude Avenue, and Virgin Mary Boulevard. A small plastic statue of Saint Anthony that was bathed in holy water and blessed by the Arch Bishop was hidden in an undisclosed location somewhere on the property to 'guarantee good fortune', according to the sales brochure. Lawsuits soon appeared because Holy Hands never constructed the paved streets, municipal sewer and water, drainage or subsurface utilities as promised and "misplaced" escrow deposits.

Frank and Vincent tried to do business at Delgado College with the approval of Dr. Demarest. They placed nearly twenty orange-colored gumball machines around campus. The signs indicated that a portion of the profits were donated to a leukemia society. According to their accounting there never were any profits. Dr. Demarest had also signed a deal with another vendor to provide food on campus including chip and drink machines. This vendor claimed that the gum machines violated the terms of his exclusive agreement. The matter was progressing in the local courts at a leisurely pace. Someone became impatient and sealed the coin mechanisms of Frank's gumball machines with super glue.

My only option was to stay in the runoff and do the best I could. Frank's mistake was admitting that he was surprised by the newspaper's editorial staff decision in my favor. The front page Election Day endorsements was the kind of support no amount of money or political support could buy and no opponent could reasonably match.

The votes in the October 25th primary as compiled by the Secretary of State were:

Dupree	57,639	40%
Demarest	38,467	27%
Jasper	29,565	21%
Scott	18,282	12%

The real politics began in the runoff and things seemed to go exactly as Frank predicted. I was now in a head-to-head election with a college president and voters would soon realize that I was an inexperienced 23 year-old college student. The Republicans hated me because I knocked out their endorsed candidate and the Democrats were eager to defeat me. I needed a miracle.

32

THINGS BEGAN TO GO DOWN hill at an astonishing fast pace. Jasper refused to endorse me and he supported Dr. Demarest instead; he was still calling for an investigation of inappropriate Dupree campaign activity. Rather than endorsing my candidacy, the Republican Party promised to introduce legislation to abolish BESE altogether at the next regular session. The Demarest Campaign began running full page ads listing accomplishments and pointing out the value of his experience. His steering committee now listed 35 of Louisiana's best known political personalities and full page newspaper ads announced his overwhelming support.

I drove to Bay Saint Louis for a meeting with Frank Bradley and David Levet. The Mississippi coastal town is about an hour's drive from New Orleans. Bay Saint Louis has served as a retreat for wealthy New Orleans residents escaping summer heat. David owned The Landmark restaurant, a converted Victorian home with a glass enclosed porch, spiraling widow's walk and ancient live oaks with Spanish moss. The afternoon sunsets over the bay were spectacular and enjoyed by locals and visitors . The Landmark was featured on the cover of *Southern Magazine* and has since enjoyed tremendous success. The difficult financial struggles for David and Doreen seemed to be in the past. "Frank is not going to make the meeting," David said. "Pick whatever you like from the menu. I suggest the Braised Trout Demoiselle De Mer and for dessert, I recommend the Creole Crepes Praline with a cup of Café Au Lait." David had a likeable friendly way. He had brownish hair and a fair completion that regularly changed to bright red. I wondered about his blood pressure. David had once been a candidate of a small New Orleans office, but withdrew shortly after qualifying. He noticed red brick dust placed in straight lines and chicken feet around his front door. "No political office was worth a voodoo curse," he said. If a person crosses a red brick line, that person is not safe from his or her enemies. Chicken feet means a curse was made. Voodoo is a relic of strange, but lingering, marriage of slave religion and Catholicism. Educated people will look down on Voodoo, but I still will not mess with Voodoo curses, nor will anyone else I know from New Orleans mess with a Voodoo curse.

"I don't like politics. But I owe Frank," said David. "He gave Doreen a job and helped finance this restaurant." I am only the messenger he reminded me. "You have one week to withdraw from the race. If you don't, then not only do you lose the Registrar offer, but Frank will work to destroy you." By this time, David's bright red complexion resembled a boiled crawfish. I could tell he was painfully uncomfortable in this arena. "Frank also asked me to mention that he noticed you did not report the RDA cash contribution on your latest finance report. He said that constitutes a violation of state campaign laws. "Just a friendly reminder," he said.

David's financial trouble began when he invested his life savings in a start up Boring and Excavation Company. An inexperience crew bored through an underground fiber optics cable causing thousands in lawsuits and repairs. Bankruptcy followed and then his marriage cracked under the financial strain. "Things are better now. I have paid back most debt and Doreen has a good job at Frank's office. The restaurant and my marriage are strong. Doreen and I may even have another child," he said raising a glass in a toast to his good fortune. David is the kind of person everyone could like. I decided to keep quiet about Frank, the Congressman, and David's wife screwing in the office and Doreen flashing her vagina to Frank's visitors. I could see David was heading for a heartbreaking crash, but I did not see anything worthwhile coming out of this for either of us, if I told him the truth. Life had a funny way throwing knockout right hooks at the most unexpected time and David seemed to have more than his fair share. I promised him that I would use The Landmark restaurant often for meetings and headed home much later than expected.

-91-

33

ANGELA CALLED ME INTO OUR den; she seemed pretty excited about something, which was not her usual, calm demeanor. She pointed towards our little television set with its snowy picture. A reporter was standing in front of Delgado College giving a dramatic report about an attempted assassination. Between what he said and what I read in the papers I think I gleaned the gist of the story.

Dr. Demarest was following his regular schedule that evening, but an unplanned meeting put him about thirty minutes behind. The would-be assassin waited across Marconi Boulevard in City Park. He had parked his Ford near the abandoned public pool behind a group of oak trees with a clear shot into the front glass wall of the Delgado gym. News cameras focused on the miniature railroad that passed within twenty feet of where the assassin had been. Apparently, the young sniper had been nervous with shaking hands and sweating profusely when he opened his door, stood up, and placed the rifle on the car's roof for a steady shot.

Andree read a detailed newspaper account that described Dr. Demarest's actions that morning. He exited the dressing room in workout clothes that once belonged to the school's baseball team and completed thirty minutes on the treadmill at a nine-minute pace. Then he used various aerobic machines for the balance of his workout time. Throughout his workout, he switched the wall mounted

TV between CNN and ESPN. The account indicated that all exercise equipment was clearly visible from the sniper's location across the Boulevard.

Later, the gunman confessed to the police that the shot was clear, but nothing happened when he squeezed the trigger. The clip was in place, a round was in the chamber. He told police that he had not released the safety. The young gunman took aim again and successfully fired the entire clip in the direction of the glass gym walls and Dr. Demarest.

Witnesses reported that the shots spun Dr. Demarest around spraying blood in a circular pattern and he fell behind a rack of free weights that saved his life. The remaining bullets expired harmlessly in walls and equipment ricocheting off the iron weights. Others in the vicinity had taken cover as they scattered in panic. A cyclist in the area fell to the ground with the presence of mind to write the license plate number in the dirt with his finger as the shooter sped away. His actions resulted in the police being able to locate the shooter.

The New Orleans Police Department did their investigative work quickly. The young shooter was arrested later that night as he sat on the front porch of his mother's Gentilly home crying with the rifle across his lap. He was a student in Delgado's Automotive Technology program. His attractive young wife was also a Delgado student working on a General Studies degree. She was the popular and beautiful president of the Student Government Association. The two of them had been high school sweethearts, married for less than two years, and were expecting their first child in four months. Earlier in the day, he learned that he was not the father of the child his wife was carrying. His ashamed wife confessed that the real father was Dr. Craig Demarest.

Dr. Demarest was not guilty of any criminal or illegal activity. However, the young husband's lawyer threatened a civil suit for loss of affection, suggested a defense of temporary insanity brought on by severe mental duress, and promised to produce evidence exposing

Delgado as a modern day Sodom and Gomorrah. "A web that will entangle the highest levels of the school's administration," he promised. Editorial pages across the area used terms like "detestable," "repulsive," and "repugnant" to describe the matter. A letter to the editor printed the next day suggested regret that the shooter's aim was poor. Bumper stickers appeared, "Defeat Demarest. The Daughter You Save May Be Your Own."

Craig Demarest's friends disappeared like ducks in an alligator pond. His wife was not surprised by his behavior, but she was stunned that he got caught. "Stupid and caviler," she said. "He had to use his position as college president to attract young girls because his penis is the size of a fifty cent roll of pennies," she said on a local TV news interview. "I hope he doesn't say he wants to retire and spend more time with his family. We don't want him!" I kept quiet and offered no comments during this "difficult time" for all concerned. The Demarest campaign was over. Although he did not formally with-draw, he did return all unused campaign donations when he realized that the funds could not be converted to his legal defense fund.

The RDA ran a full page ad in the City Business weekly paper, "Andre Dupree and the Old Regulars. Louisiana's Youngest Political Candidate and Oldest Political Organization Working Together for Positive Change." Most groups pulled their support of Demarest with most printing apologies expressing their embarrassment and regret. The newspaper reprinted their Dupree endorsement. Election Day official returns showed:

Dupree	70,844	64%
Demarest	39,271	36%

The election night victory party was held at our small rental home. The Campaign Committee expected a dozen or so guests, but over one hundred and fifty well wishers showed up. Food ran out quickly until someone ordered dozens of pizzas. Media from television and radio were requesting interviews, how did they know where to find me? "We are here with political newcomer, Andre Dupree, on the eve of a convincing victory. Mr. Dupree how do you feel?" they asked.

It was an amazing night although the fact that I actually won had not set in fully. However, I did feel a little let down. After working so hard for so long, the victory was nearly anti-climatic. Dr. Demarest called to offer congratulations. I tried to make my way quickly through the crowds, but when I finally reached the telephone he had already hung-up. I wish I had talked with Demarest since I would be making a similar call to my opponent on the eve of her victory as my promising political career collapsed with astonishing speed. I do not remember very much more from this night, wish I did, it was the time of my life.

Member- Louisiana State Board of
Elementary and Secondary Education

34

I WAS NOT SCHEDULED TO be sworn in until February along with all other newly elected state office holders. However, a sitting BESE member that had not run for re-election resigned in early December leaving an unexpired seat open for about three months. The Governor appointed me to finish that unexpired term, one of the very few Republican appointments that he ever made.

The state trooper standing at the front door of the Governor's Mansion said I was expected and showed me to a large waiting room off to the left. Two troopers were stationed here at all times. They sat in a small room off to the right that housed weapons and communications gear. An elderly black man dressed in a starched white Department of Corrections uniform served coffee and fresh fruit grown at the Angola State Prison. "Yes sir. Yes sir," was all he said. As a Creole, I felt torn..

The floor was covered by a thick wool rug with the Great Seal of Louisiana in the middle. The Governor entered the room alone and although it was 2:00 PM on a Wednesday, he was dressed in pajamas. He preferred to work from the small office at the mansion or his private law office, using the Capital Building only when the legislature was in session. He removed the appointment proclamation from a cardboard tube and signed it on his lap. The signature appears shaky because he did not have a solid writing surface. "We will get along fine," he said. I appreciated the early appointment since it gave me a head start over the other newly elected members and time to learn the position and the inner workings. I promised to take the Governor's calls and consider his position on upcoming issues. He assured me that good things would follow for players who stayed on his team.

I invited Dan to dinner at his favorite steak house on Ferret Street, I owed him. "It's not often that an elected official offers to pick up the tab on my dinner," he said. "You did an amazing job. How does it feel to win?" Things had happened so fast that I really did not yet take the time to enjoy it.

"I do hope Delgado College was not damaged in all this. Delgado is important to the city and its people." Dan provided tuition waivers to his employees. Most attended Delgado and earned two year degrees and went on to the University of New Orleans to complete four year degrees. At any time, Dan may have been covering tuition expenses for fifteen part-time students. He did not believe in dead ends and wanted his employees to have other opportunities when the time came to part ways.

"Dan you rascal! Did you have anything to do with all this?" He explained again that everything is always about sex.

"You should write a book," I said.

"I am amazed by the things men will tell their prostitute friends. I asked my girls at Delgado to get to know Demarest. That's all. He really believed he was a ladies' man. He made it so easy. Didn't even realize they were playing him. Demarest was a fool, the weakest man in the room," Dan responded.

35

THE VERY NEXT DAY I met Mr. Tanner at the Sazerac Restaurant in the Fairmont Hotel. He ate lunch there nearly every day at a private table in the corner supplied with fresh red roses. He wore a heavy, loose fitting gold bracelet that made a sound like coins dropping on the table each time he pounded his fist. "You ran one hell of a race, Andre! How does a 23 year-old political unknown peel the bark off three experienced politicians, including a college president?" He was not expecting an answer. "Do you have any campaign debt that we need to take care of?"

I explained the campaign surplus of a few hundred dollars was donated to a scholarship fund (Pelican Association) at Tulane in the name of Dr. Barrilleaux.

"He helped develop your campaign strategy, correct?" he asked. "I have studied his ideas and need to meet him," Mr. Tanner said.

Nora Davis was the Chief of Administration at Tanner Energy Company and always at Paul Tanner's side. She was tall and beautiful. Her husband was an oil field supply salesman and held key sales contracts with Tanner Energy providing drilling pipe and bits. "Your BESE district is the exact same as the Congressional 1st District. Do you realize that? Do you realize that you ran stronger in this District than Congressman Lynchard? Lynchard blames oil and gas for Louisiana's coastal erosion problems. This CEWL(Coastal Environmental Wetlands Levy) proposal of his will cost my company millions." Mr. Tanner slammed his fist down so hard that patrons on the other side of the restaurant were startled. We spent the next twenty minutes discussing Congressman Lynchard. I kept quiet about the Congressman's regular visits with Frank and Doreen and their threesomes.

A moment of awkward silence followed. Mr. Tanner finished the vodka on the rocks and stared in my direction. "You will work for Tanner Energy. What do you need?" I was not expecting a job offer.

"I hadn't thought about a career with your company Mr. Tanner. Can I think about this for a time?"

He ordered vodka for everyone at the table. "No you can't. I don't have time. What do you want?" He asked again looking straight at me.

Eye contact was unsettling because he could go long intervals without blinking; I stared at his forehead just above the eyes. I knew what I wanted, but was hesitant to ask. I gathered my courage, "Mr. Tanner, I want a healthy salary and one more thing," I said.

"What is it?" he asked.

"Well, Mr. Tanner, I want a Tulane education."

"Done!" He slammed his gold bracelets on the table. "Nora will call the university tomorrow. You start at Tanner Energy on Monday." We stood to shake hands and the bodyguards reappeared.

"Welcome aboard, Andre," they said with a slap on my back. We walked towards the hotel lobby where Mr. Tanner and Nora entered a small elevator that went directly to a private suite. The body guards stood at attention on each side of the elevator door. Mr. Tanner and Nora took two-hour lunches regularly. The first hour was spent at the Sazerac restaurant and the second was spent in the suite.

36

THE UNEXPECTED OFFER OF A lucrative job and a Tulane education had my sprits high, but looming before me was my first introduction to the reality of Louisiana politics. My first BESE meeting was scheduled for the following Thursday. Committee meetings were always held on the third Tuesday and Wednesday of each month and the full board met on Thursday. The State Department of Education building is a product of the 1970's urban renewal movement, an unremarkable cement structure with inadequate air conditioning and much deferred maintenance sitting across from the Capital building with a view of Huey Long's grave. The top two floors are occupied by the Superintendent and his deputies. The BESE offices and meeting rooms are located on the second floor along with a government-sponsored deli. The superintendent's office was spread over two floors with a spiral staircase and private marble bath. The BESE offices were neglected with worn carpets and yellowed ceiling tiles. Faux leather chairs, used in the meeting rooms, were torn at the seams and the padding removed from the arms in order for the chairs to fit under the mismatched tables.

I had not been issued a parking pass, but managed to find a spot near the capital and walked the two blocks. Nervous and unsure where to go, I was surprised by the large number of people milling about. A Vo-Tech director recognized me and announced my presence. I received dozens of business cards, handshakes, pats on the back and dinner invitations. "Mr. Dupree it is great to finally meet.

We have been expecting you. Please follow me. The BESE Executive Director would like to say hello."

I was ushered into the office of Alice Theriot. She was older and showed the poise of someone who had witnessed many battles, but it was clear the struggles had taken a toll. Ms. Theriot rose from behind her desk and seemed pleased to meet. "We are here to help you. My staff is yours." For the next few minutes we discussed routine matters in a brief orientation. I handed her a list of my appointments required for the various boards and organizations. I appointed Dan to a commission overseeing cultural arts education in the public schools. David Levet would help oversee culinary arts programs offered at the Vo-Techs and Phillip Freiberg would help review grant proposals. Phillip had organized the Jasper volunteer sign crew. He graduated with an accounting degree and now had a fantastic job with the Comptroller of the Currency as a bank auditor.

Along the walls of Theriot's office were family size bags of Ruffles potato chips. Most bags were open but few chips were eaten. On her desk was a small bowl with about ten regular chips. "Ms. Phillips will take you to the private area where members gather before meeting. The others should already be here. The meeting will start at 10:00 AM," she said as I was escorted out.

We walked maybe forty feet when the relative tranquility was shattered by a series of ear piercing screams. "I found one! I found one!" over again. "I found one!" This was followed by a whooping cry of excitement and feet stomping. I recognized the exuberant voice as that of Alice Theriot. "Don't be alarmed" Ms. Philips said. She explained that Alice relives stress by hunting through bags of potato chips to find a regular chip inadvertently packed in a Ruffle bag.

The BESE members were gathered in the private meeting room enjoying coffee and doughnuts. I was introduced to BESE members John Honoree from Crowley, Carson Boyer and Keith Hayes. John Honoree's brother had a high ranking position within the Transportation Bureau of the Department of Education. The cooperation between the two brothers often raised eyebrows. John attempted to force a vote requiring all Louisiana public school buses to have their roofs painted with a special and unique heat reflective paint. "Guaranteed to lower interior bus temperature by 25 degrees," according to John. He also promoted an effort to require the installation of automatic air pressure gauges on all bus tires, which experts claimed, according to John, would lower fuel consumption by 5%.

At his advanced age John Honoree's interests focused more on his son now, State Senator John Jr. Some newspapers gave John Jr. a good chance in the next Governor's race, before the indictment and jail term did him in, that is. Jr. claimed he never accepted payoffs from gambling interest. He did however have a Gulf Shores condominium that he rented to the lobbyist for $30,000 per week. The going rate at the time was about $2,500. The ensuing trial and conviction ended his political aspirations.

BESE members that had been defeated in recent elections did not bother to attend these final meetings making it difficult to reach a quorum. This was the December meeting anyhow and various schools from around the state were invited to perform for the state board, nothing much in terms of real business was expected. The young children from the Louisiana School for the Deaf performed a Christmas drama. After the performance I reviewed the agenda and was surprised to see items calling for the election of a Board President. It was highly unusual for an outgoing body to address important issues unless they were trying to tie the hands of the new incoming Board.

"I am not prepared to vote for BESE president today," I informed Keith. He said it made no difference anyway because he had six votes to be elected Board President. "It made no difference what I did," he said. Keith did say a unanimous vote for him as President would be appreciated. "I can't do that. I don't want to vote for anything with a new Board set to begin in two months," I said.

BESE members sit in a semi-circle behind a curved wooden table and faced a fire ordinance capacity of nearly two hundred and fifty. Directly behind my chair was a door that led to a passage way to an underground parking area. This design allowed for quick escapes. The meeting was called to order with the pledge and a prayer. Holiday greetings were exchanged from various state agencies including the Book Depository and the Vocational Educational Council. Next agenda item was the election of Board Officers. I was prepared to express logical reasons for requesting a delay of consideration.

Since it was the holiday week and everyone was eager to get back to their families a motion was made by John Honoree to consider all agenda items in "global." As acting President Keith had the floor. "I have a motion. Do I have a second?" The motion was seconded by Carson Boyer. "I have a motion and second," Keith said. "Any discussion? All in favor? Any opposed? Motion carries!" The next motion was to adjoun. The meeting was over before I figured out how to use the microphone.

Keith walked over to my chair and thanked me for not opposing his Presidency. "The unanimous vote is appreciated," he said and offered the Chairmanship of the Vocational Education Committee and Due Process Committee. The Vo-Tech Committee oversaw the operation and administration of the statewide job training system. Due Process settled all employee grievances that could not be handled at the local level. I was thrilled to have important chairmanships as a freshman member and unaware that other members turned these committee assignments down as undesirable.

I answered reporter's questions regarding my perceived good fortune with landing important committee assignments. However, Louisiana's economy is driven by oil and the price had recently dropped to $12 per barrel. The state was teetering on bankruptcy. Drastic Vo-Tech budget cut proposals calling for numerous school closings and the resulting Reduction In Force (RIF) plans would overwhelm the Due Process Committee for years.

The New York Times ran articles about Louisiana's economic quagmire. With so many people leaving Louisiana, one-way moving companies had to convoy moving trucks back in. Normally, a natural balance is maintained between trucks coming into a state and those moving out. Not so at this time in Louisiana. Residents frequently witnessed the eerie sight of dozens of U-Haul trucks convoyed into Louisiana's southern cities, satisfying the needs of those trying to get out of the state.

The day rates for oil field supply boats, crew boats, jack up rigs, and tow boats fell below operational costs. In the Cutoff and LaRose area of Bayou Lafourche, boat storage yards were full to capacity with the depreciated assets of now bankrupt companies. A former LSU football all star invested his fortune in a small supply boat company. All six purple and gold boats of "Tiger Fleet" were now in, what is known as, moth balls at a storage yard along with dozens of other boats. Property values were low as a flood of For Sale signs hit the market. Somehow, it became my responsibility to deliver important job training vocational skills necessary for Louisiana's economic recovery and stabilization just two years after *Fortune* magazine discussed the incredible oil wealth flowing into the state.

37

I WAS BACK AT THE Tanner Energy office completing the necessary employment paperwork, W-2, insurance, and 401K. My office was across the hall from Mr. Tanner's, behind the visitor waiting area. I met my new secretary Joann from Belize. After I completed the paperwork, I drove to Tulane's campus to see Dr. Barrilleaux and register as a part-time Tulane University college student. He carefully reviewed my University of New Orleans transcript and compared course descriptions. "Andre you are very close to completing a BA Degree at UNO, maybe less than one semester. Tulane will not accept all your UNO credits. To earn a Tulane degree you will almost start over." I knew that. It did not matter. He continued, "Each course here is worth four credit hours; UNO's are three, so you will need about eleven courses. That represents nearly a four to five year commitment to night and weekend studies. What about your obligations to Mr. Tanner and what about BESE? Wouldn't it be wise to simply complete the UNO degree?" he asked.

Dr. Barrilleaux opened a desk drawer and removed a dark green binder with the gold Tulane crest embossed on the cover. "However, if you manage to complete the work, this is what you will have earned." He slid the binder across the desk in my direction. I picked it up and opened it slowly. I had never seen a Tulane degree. "On the recommendation of the Faculty————-Have this day conferred upon." I can do this. What ever it takes, I will.

I hurried back, eager to return to Tanner Energy in time to attend Mr. Tanner's weekly officer's conference. This was the first time I attended a corporate meeting at this level and wondered how top executives conduct business. The meeting was held in the large board room at the center of the office area. Tables were arranged in a U pattern with Mr. Tanner sitting at the front in order for him to see all his corporate leaders at once. He would move down the line asking each executive about his or her department. I had the last seat to his left and watched the meeting progress as he pointed his finger one by one around the room getting closer to me. I had no idea what I would say, but he never got that far.

He reviewed the Year over Year or "YOY" drilling plans and asked for any concerns or objections. "I need leaders willing to stand up. What good are a bunch of yes men?" Mr. Tanner asked.

Don, the Director of Purchasing took the bait. "Mr. Tanner I wonder how wise is it to undertake an ambitious and expensive drilling schedule at the current time." He then presented a long list of economic concerns.

"Thank you for speaking your mind. Does anyone else agree with Don?" No one stepped forward. "Well, at least one of you has testicles. Thank you Don." While it is one thing to disagree with the leader in a private setting, another altogether to do it in public. Next week Don was fired for allegedly demanding kickbacks from drilling supply salesman, an internal investigation was launched.

On one side of the office complex was Mr. Tanner's office, his secretary, and my office. There was also a small board room to the back and the visitors and reception area in the front. The legal department was across a hall from the small board room. A PR office was adjacent. To the left was an employee kitchen that opened to the large meeting area used for the officers' meetings. On the other side was the work area. The geology department, purchasing, maintenance, aviation, and accounting were all located on this side.

The evening before, Mr. Tanner visited with production staff then used the bathroom. While washing his hands, the water shut off. The faucets were spring loaded and set to shut off after a short time, like airport faucets. "I am the richest man in Louisiana and can't afford water for employees to wash their hands," he cursed. Tanner called his head of maintenance, John. He wore a blue cotton shirt with dark blue pants. An American flag patch was on the right shoulder and his name was embossed over his left pocket along with the Tanner, "T." John had worked for Tanner Energy for fifteen years and never advanced. He was in charge of the office cleaning staff and an all around handy man. "John, you have these faucet springs removed today or you will be fired tomorrow! Understand?" Mr. Tanner was serious. He once fired an employee for having one misspelling in a draft letter. John called the plumber and the springs were removed that evening. John inspected the completed work himself.

At the weekly meeting, Mr. Tanner continued to make his way around the room asking questions of each executive. He eventually reached John. "Did you have those faucets repaired?"

John responded with confidence. "Yes sir, Mr. Tanner. Checked it myself yesterday."

Mr. Tanner smiled. "Why don't we all go have a look?" Everyone rose up and followed John and Mr. Tanner to the bathroom. "Try it, John," Mr. Tanner said. John turned the faucet clockwise and in five seconds the water automatically shut off. He tried again with the same unexpected results, shut off!

"Mr. Tanner, please. I don't understand. I checked it myself. It was fixed, exactly as you ordered." John folded his hands together as if to pray. "I need my job, Mr. Tanner. Please!" I noticed a smirk on Mr. Tanner's face and some of the others. John continued to beg and plead for his job, "I have three children!"

John did not know that Mr. Tanner called the plumber and had the springs reinstalled that morning. "All in fun," Tanner said to John with a slap on the back.

38

THE GOVERNOR BEGAN MAKING HIS appointments to the state education boards. I met his three BESE appointments for the first time after the Christmas meetings. Mrs. Theus Haute from Tioga was named to BESE first. Theus and her husband, Reverend Brother Haute, were the leaders of the Louisiana Pentecostal Convention. Each year, five to ten thousand Pentecostal faithful gather in the pine woods around Tioga for an annual revival celebration. Elected officials and political hopefuls lobbied for Brother Haute's permission to address the gathering and kiss political ass.

Dr. Huel Pickens, the governor's best appointment, was a Liberal Arts professor at LSU and had been named Louisiana Humanitarian of the year in 1989. He was a very serious man, but possessed a wonderful sense of humor. A commercial arts teacher from a Monroe Vocational College brought her class to a BESE meeting to defend the program's funding. The students occupied the first row of seats across the front. The teacher rose to the podium. An attractive blond student wearing a short skirt and sitting directly in front of Dr. Pickens and me began opening and closing her legs while licking her lips. Dr. Pickens watched for a while then turned off his microphone leaned over and whispered, "Andre, how can we vote against that? I don't care how broke this state is!" He turned the microphone back on and made a motion to restore funding. I offered the second.

Loselle Dearmond, the third appointment, was also a college professor with strong ties to the black community in the Baton Rouge area. She gained statewide name recognition when the *Evening Advocate* newspaper claimed that she used federal funds for inappropriate travel junkets around the country and Europe. As a result, the U.S. Department of Education conducted an audit and confirmed the inappropriate spending. BESE was presented with a bill for $756,605. In another matter, Loselle's husband was transferred from a regular teaching post by Webster Parish School officials to a new special position created after BESE approved funding of a seven parish special educational consortium. Loselle said that her husband's hiring was a local decision and not in any way influenced by her BESE position. "I would choose to hope not because that would be a tremendous blow to his ego," she said.

I was also getting to know the newly elected BESE members better. Carson Boyer from Port Vincent was a former aid to Congressman Gillis Long representing the 8th Congressional District. When Gillis died in office, Carson was expected to win the special election to fill the unexpired term until Kathy Long, Gillis's widow, entered the race and won the sympathy vote. Carson ran fifth in the five person primary election and received only 12% of the vote and an $85,000 unpaid campaign debt.

As a teenager, Carson and friends found little to do for entertainment in rural Louisiana, so created their own. They trapped jack rabbits, put the rabbits in old suitcases, and strategically place the suitcases alongside county roads. Travelers would pass, spot the suitcase, slow down, reverse back and pick up, what they thought, was a found prize. Usually the driver would look around, jump out quickly, grab the suitcase, and speed off. Carson and friends would follow behind waiting for the moment when the frightened rabbit was liberated from the suitcase. "Funny as hell." he said.

Carson purchased a new Lincoln and was eager to show off his new car. He lived in a wooded area on about 10 acres. In the evenings, he placed the garbage on top of the trunk of his old car and drove to the front gate in the morning, placing the trash in the cans before heading to Baton Rouge. Living in a wooded areas as he did, this method was the best way to keep the critters from getting into his garbage at night. However, he did not want to damage the paint on the new Lincoln, instead, on the evening before garbage pickup, he carefully placed the trash in the trunk.

The next morning, forgetting about the change in routine with the garbage, Carson drove past his gate and headed to the BESE meeting. By lunch, the car had been sitting in the scorching Louisiana heat for four hours. "Wait till you see these leather seats," he said proudly. The stench was overwhelming reminding me of the road kill episode during qualifying. Smells can easily revive old memories like that.

"I love that new car smell," said John jokingly. "Sure am glad I bought a Volvo." Carson removed the garbage bags, but the juices had leaked out and seeped thoroughly into the trunk carpeting and insulation. Later from the BESE office, I looked out and saw Carson parked near a dumpster tearing out the trunk material with one hand and holding a handkerchief over his nose with the other.

Carson used BESE campaign funds to repay personal loans for his unsuccessful congressional race. He solicited campaign donations from employees of the State Department of Education, from firms that do business with BESE, and from people linked to schools regulated by BESE and Vo-Tech Directors. "I can't control why people give. I can only control how I act to the people that do," he said. Some said they voted for Carson out of sympathy because he seemed unlucky in politics. They would not support him for Congress, but figured he was harmless on BESE.

Marie Snodgrass was from Monroe and had been one of the first female attorneys in the Parish. She won a BESE seat after retiring from the practice of law and has been reelected a few times; she was nearly 80 years old. The family made a fortune from Delta Airlines stock. Delta was founded in Monroe as a small crop dusting enterprise in the 1920's and the early investors did quite well. South Louisiana had oil, Northeast Louisiana had Delta Airlines.

The Snodgrass family lived along the banks of the Mississippi River in a former country club that they converted into a private mansion. Marie loved dogs and at least five large hounds had free run of the house. These dogs were her favorites and considered family members. Other dogs lived outside on the property and roamed the old golf course. John Honoree had business in Monroe and accepted an invitation to stay at the Snodgrass estate. Dinner was served in the formal dining room. John pretended not to notice Marie feeding left-overs to the hounds from dinner plates.

After dinner John had a pleasant time discussing politics and sipping cognac while the hounds rested on a wool rug in front of the parlor fireplace. John retired to his bedroom after the staff had turned down the sheets of the canopy bed and warmed the room with a fire in the stone fireplace. The bathroom was situated two doors down the hall on the right. John awoke early, before dawn, put on a robe, and proceeded to the bathroom. The others were awakened by a loud crash and John's cries for assistance. They found him flat on his back-side. "God damn it! Son of a bitch!" he was not hurt, but was mad as hell. The combination of fresh dog crap on polished wood floors, John's bare feet ,and his shifting weight produced a slippery effect pro-pelling him across the hall. The force of his backwards crash was felt throughout the house.

Dorothy Roper was a member of the Desoto Parish School Board for 16 years and was a past president of the Louisiana School Boards Association. Her family's financial success was made hauling North Louisiana timber. Against my better judgment, I agreed to help Frank Bradley get new business for AMTC. While I did not mention Frank's name, I asked Dorothy for help securing trucking routes. She requested truck serial numbers and descriptions, both of which I provided. The next week I received a call from a reporter in Baton Rouge, "How does someone from your limited financial background become wealthy so fast? Each truck you own is valued at $225,000," he asked.

"If you think I own those trucks then prove it!" I said. However, I should have known better than to trust any of these people.

Dorothy was nearly forced to resign when she told a racist joke that forced a public apology and statewide outcry. Her political survival was important to the Governor. I lied to the *Picayune Journal* reporter by explaining that my support of Dorothy was in return for her support of nonpublic school funding. The story was a logical and a believable fabrication since my District contained many private and Catholic schools. Dorothy supported my version of events and confirmed nonpublic funding plans when she joined with Keith to have me named Chairman of the Finance Committee. This committee is the King Pin of all committees because it controlled most funding, including the $1.9 billion dollar Minimum Foundation Program. Dr. Pickens said that he could not remain on a board with Dorothy's racist leadership and resigned.

39

HAVING BEEN TOO POOR FOR too long I was ready to try and make real money. I understood there was a clear correlation between politics and wealth, but not really sure how that all worked out. I was happy with my Tanner salary but wanted more. Tanner called his level of wealth "liquid" having the money to do whatever he wanted, whenever. Don't miss understand, I didn't want to do anything illegal and I really didn't want to be 'liquid," I only wanted to live, for once, without financial stress.

I happened to meet members of the Mississippi State Board of Education. They were enthusiastic because they believed casino gambling revenue would be used to improve Mississippi's underfunded public schools. "We will have computers in every 1st grade classroom statewide," they said. The gambling legislation had not been introduced or publicly discussed, but the board members had internal polls showing if done correctly, a gambling measure could pass. The proposal would include casinos built on giant barges scatted along the entire Mississippi coast from Louisiana to Alabama.

Hurricane Camille hit this area in 1969 with 200 mph winds and massive destruction, the Mississippi coastal economy never recovered. Gulf front property remained undervalued for nearly 20 years with little incentive for any economic improvement. "I think we can make some money. Want to take a little risk?" I asked Angela. We had a small nest egg set aside from my Tanner salary, Angela was unsure.

"Let's just take a look," I convinced her. We drove to the Pass Christian area and met a real estate agent who was eager to sell.

"This will be my first sale this month," he said.

We made on offer on the first property we saw, 411 feet on the beach and 75 feet deep, the asking price was $25,000 and we offered $21,000. The beach highway runs between the sandy beach and the property, most of the actual Mississippi beach is publicly owned, but this property had been in the same family since the Civil War and 411 feet of beach rights were included in the transaction. The agent called the owners.

"Andre, they accepted your $21,000 offer and agreed to owner financing with a 10% down payment and a 5 year note." We closed the following month.

Within five months, the Mississippi Legislature passed a gambling law. Major gambling interest from Nevada and New Jersey began buying everything in sight. I listed the property for $225,000 and expected to negotiate substantially. Realistically, I expected a sale price around $150,000. When I arrived back in New Orleans, the phone was ringing. "I have a 100% cash offer, full price!" The excited agent explained. "They want to close this week! Cash money, Andre!"

I could not believe this good fortune and didn't want the buyers to back out. "Let them have the beach rights. Throw that in as well," I told the agent, hoping to cement the deal.

"Andre, they have not asked for the rights. They don't even know they exist." However, I insisted believing it was the right thing to do.

"OK, but I disagree,' the agent said reluctantly.

I made more money than I ever imagined and felt like a real estate tycoon. Mississippi gambling became a huge success; the coast became a rival to Las Vegas. The beach rights today are worth millions and I gave them away! I suspect that in some Nevada boardroom a group of executives are smoking cigars and having a good laugh at my expense, "What was that kid's name that gave away beach rights?" Nevertheless, I managed to make a substantial profit and Angela and I purchased our first home, a 1900's cottage in St. Tammany, and I could live without financial stress, my original goal after all.

40

I ALWAYS ARRIVED AT THE Tanner Energy office early. The quiet time was relaxing and I enjoyed an early cup of coffee with chicory and the morning newspaper. I read the editorial pages first and then moved on to the Metro section. Mr. Tanner came in from the Foxworth Mississippi ranch on Monday and usually arrived around 10:00 AM. The runway in Foxworth was short so Paul used the Maul, a small single prop plane capable of very short takeoffs and landings. The Maul could land at the ranch, avoiding the need for an airport altogether. However, Paul's favorite ranch was 30,000 acres in New Mexico and he used the Kingair 300 or Falcon 9 for these longer flights.

Paul Tanner had stayed in New Orleans this weekend so he was due in around 7:30 AM. I was enjoying my coffee reading about the mayor's race with my feet on the desk when the sound of pistol shots reverberated through the building. I spilled hot coffee and fell to the floor behind my desk. The guards usually escorted Mr. Tanner to the 5th floor office, made sure he was safely inside, and then returned to secure the automobiles. At this time, Mr. Tanner would be alone. After the pistol shot, things were quiet for a while so I slowly made my way towards Paul's office. The door frame was splintered and the knob was shot off. Paul was behind his desk looking over reports. "Are you alright?" I asked.

"Yes, I told the cleaning crew that I want this door unlocked when I arrive. How difficult is that to understand?" Paul Tanner considered shooting the door easier than using a key, I guess. Or maybe this was his way of making a point. "By the way," he continued as if nothing happened. "We need to be at Livingston Middle School this morning at 9:00 AM." He said that we might just shake things up. "Andre, you don't mind if I steal your ideas, do you?" he asked.

I decided to drive my own car since I had a Baton Rouge meeting later that day and would not have time to go back to the Tanner office. Livingston Middle was in New Orleans East on Dwyer Road in a poor area of the city. Crime was common and nearly all the students were free lunch eligible and considered at risk for dropping out of school . Most students were not even expected to make it to high school.

Adjacent to the Tanner office was the parking garage. Attendants had the cars waiting with the engines running. Paul would walk out the building and into his waiting car and driven off in a matter of seconds. His Mercedes 600 pulled out first and I followed closely behind and two additional guards followed behind me in a Chevy Impala. We drove over the Industrial Canal Bridge, along Downman Road and turned onto Dwyer Road. "Don't ever do that again!" said Dennis, the head of security for Tanner Energy, he was upset about something.

"What?" I asked.

Dennis carried so much gear, weapons, ammo and radios that I often wondered how his pants stayed up. He was using his hands to describe driving maneuvers. Each hand represented a car. When he raised his arm his jacket opened and I notice one 9mm on his hip and another in a holster strapped under his armpit. Dennis demonstrated the importance of security "agents" staying directly behind the lead auto. My mistake was getting between Paul's Mercedes and security following in the second car.

41

DENNIS HAD BEEN A PATROLMAN with the Jefferson Parish Sheriff's Office making a living writing tickets and escorting weddings before becoming Tanner Energy Chief of Security. He traveled with us to Washington DC when Paul had meetings with the Commandant of the Marine Corps in the Pentagon. Earlier, Dennis advised Paul to carry a small caliber handgun concealed in a leather billfold when traveling and Dennis arranged for the proper permits. Paul Tanner walked through the Pentagon security check first, Dennis and I were trailing. The X-ray machines were manned by armed Marines, some Marines stood at attention near the entrance, and some inspected items placed in trays. Paul was a fast walker and was starting to move down the hall when the red lights began flashing and alarms sounded. Two large doors swung open in a violent manner as a company of assault trained Marines with automatic weapons burst into the hall forming a human barricade with enough firepower to stop a tank. The Marines stood between the entrance and the corridors with laser sights trained on Mr. Tanner. "On the floor, now! On the floor!" they yelled. A Marine had his foot on Mr. Tanner's head and others had their knees in his back. All of them were yelling at him not to move.

"I have a permit to carry," Mr. Tanner cried. "Check my wallet," he said.

"You have a firearms permit from the Orleans Parish Civil Sheriff!" the Marine Officer asked.

"Yes sir, that's right" Mr. Tanner replied.

"Are you crazy? Do you know where you are? This is the Pentagon!" the Officer said as he placed his weapon's safety back on.

The Washington trip was memorable for another reason. We returned to the Watergate Hotel late that night after a series of successful meetings. "We had a long day. Andre, take this and enjoy yourself." Paul handed me $300 dollars. I loosened my tie, crossed the lobby and walked over to a quiet bar. The hotel was owned by the Conard Line and was decorated with a nautical theme reflecting the company's glorious heritage. Behind the bar was an eight foot long shipyard scale replica of the Queen Mary. I ordered a Long Island Tea that cost $25 and looked over at the attractive women sitting alone drinking Scotch and reviewing papers held in a metal briefcase. She smiled, motioned for me to come over, and closed the briefcase as I approached.

I caught a glimpse inside her case and noticed the Senate ID badge. "I wanted to meet the person that can drink Long Island Teas. I'm Cyndi. Have I met you before?" she asked confidently.

"Don't think so. I'm from New Orleans and haven't been here before," I said. We talked about politics. "I'm sorry, but I didn't catch your name," she asked and held out her hand again, but did not let go quickly. "Dupree, Andre Dupree."

She grasped her left hand over my right and held tightly, staring directly into my eyes. "Are you kidding? You must be kidding," she asked. Cyndi had been reading a romance novel where the beautiful young antebellum belle slips out of her family's plantation home escaping her mundane life in the arms of a Creole lover. "His name was Dupree! Dupree, French Creole, just like you!"

Making friends with Cyndi was erotic and memorable and her Senate job would prove helpful once the Federal Election Commission threatened to charge me with felony election finance fraud. This passionate romance would light a fire in my memory that still burns hot, she shares these feelings. Cyndi would risk a lucrative career to help me. I constantly wonder why she would wager so much on my behalf and wonder if I was worthy of such unselfish affection.

42

OUR MOTORCADE ARRIVED AT LIVINGSTON Middle School prepared for Mr. Tanner's 9:00 AM talk, but the correct time was actually 10:00 AM. Lakefront Airport is about a ten-minute drive from the school. Paul was aggravated about the time confusion, but enjoyed visiting the airport. He had not yet purchased a personal hanger so his planes were stored at the MillionAir facility where crews maintained aircraft and prepared aircraft for flight on short notice. What Paul really wanted to see was his newest acquisition, a perfectly restored Korean War era Sky Raider, a fighter bomber with a single radial engine, capable of carrying a larger payload than a B-17.

The MillionAir employees prepared to start the proud old war bird's engine. They instructed us to stand back. "The young Marines and 7th Infantry Army soldiers were retreating from the Chosin Reservoir area in near zero degree temperatures with three hundred thousand screaming Chinese and North Koreans on their tails." Paul explained. "The American retreat was orderly as the Marine and Army columns moved south performing rear guard maneuvers. They were outnumbered and constantly harassed by Communists trying to cut them off," Paul said. We were given ear plugs. Paul put his in his pocket. "For our boys on the ground their only hope was brave Marine pilots and these Sky Raiders. They flew at tree top level, in formations of six, over the retreating American columns; the ground trembled under the pounding of their pistons. Raining punishment down upon the Communist with everything this aircraft could deliver. On return, they flew low over the retreating Marines, this time rocking their wings back and forth, in the traditional airman's victory symbol to the cheers of the desperate soldiers on the frozen ground. They landed; pilots stayed in the cockpits, engine running, ground crews refueled and rearmed, and they took off again and again. They kept coming and coming, Marines never give up. That is why I love this airplane so," Paul said.

Paul's passion for history was obvious. He viewed history as important recognition of past accomplishments. The massive Pratt and Whitney engine roared to life. Paul was lost in thought. "We are going to do something significant today. We are going to make history today by changing education forever! Andre, did you ever think your campaign ideas would actually be taken seriously? Just watch!" He said as we headed back to Livingston Middle School.

43

DR. MARIE COLLINS WAS DIRECTOR of the At-Risk programs at Livingston Middle. She had offered her name repeatedly as a Republican candidate for the Orleans Parish School Board, but was unsuccessful each time. Dr. Collins and Paul met through her political activities and, as a black female Republican, she was as unique as snow days in New Orleans. When we entered the school, Marie was waiting at the entrance with a small group of well dressed students. I assumed these were the best and brightest. The students gave Paul flowers and directed us towards the auditorium where 221 At Risk students were waiting.

Marie rose to the podium introducing Paul; however, most students seemed uninterested. She believed in iron fist discipline but "with a velvet glove," she said. When she clapped her hands, the students sat up straight. I was standing against a wall towards the back where I had an overall view of the group. Two students had been fondling each other under their coats that lay across their laps. At the sound of Dr. Collin's voice, they folded their arms and sat upright.

"Students," she started. "We have a very special treat today. Mr. Paul Tanner started out poor. He did not know his father and his mother was a secretary. He struggled to get an education and become an oil man," she said. Paul was standing on the edge of the stage. He pulled out a piece of paper, read over it, and placed it back in his pocket. "Today he is the richest man in Louisiana and owns Tanner

Energy Company, the largest independent Oil and Gas Company in Louisiana. Students, please welcome Mr. Paul Tanner." The students clapped with little enthusiasm as Paul stepped to the podium.

"My circumstances were very similar to your own. Some would say even worse. At 15, I was on my own, working part-time while attending school. I worked hard and won a scholarship to a prestigious private high school in Houston. In 1986, I won the Horatio Alger award recognizing rags to riches accomplishment. I am the richest man in this state, in fact one of the richest in the entire country." I think Paul knew that a "you can do it, too" speech would have little effect on students that had already failed twice and had little chance of finishing high school.

"I am not here to brag. I am here today to present an offer. I succeeded because at sometime during my life, someone believed in me and those positive expectations drove me to succeed." He explained more about expectations as an important component of a prosperous life. "I believe in each of you," he said. "If you stay in school, take college preparatory classes, maintain a B average, and stay out of trouble, then I will see to it that each of you will go to college!"

A former Chairman of the State Republican Party told a different story about Mr. Tanner's upbringing. "Paul's mother was a secretary for John W. Miller Sr. Paul was on his own at 15 years old because his father found out that Paul was the product of a long term affair between his wife and John Miller Sr. Paul thought he won scholarships; but in reality the tuition was always secretly covered by John Miller. Paul's first job after college was with a Miller company, creating tension between Paul and John Miller Jr. John Jr. would become owner of a New Orleans professional football team. Paul was always trying to top that. Paul's first company, Square Bar Drilling, was funded by Mr. Miller Sr. "All this stuff about being a self-made man is a bunch of crap," the Chairman said. You can never be sure what motivates people, but that is what he said nonetheless.

44

REGARDLESS OF THE TRUTHFULNESS OF his life story, Paul's deal with the students generated much needed excitement in an educationally bankrupt school system. News crews were requesting interviews with Paul and Marie Collins. The students now called "Tanner Kids" appeared on local morning talk shows and Paul was getting the notoriety his ego demanded. His offer to provide college tuition was already discussed as a possible state-wide program. Media began calling the concept the "Tanner Plan." However, some community leaders, such as the President of Southern University — New Orleans said that the Tanner offer was useless because it did not address the problems of drugs, violence, poverty, and homelessness.

Dr. Wilmer Culver, State Superintendent of Education, told the paper that the Tanner offer would do nothing that "Pell Grants, Student Loans and existing scholarships cannot do." He also said that "about 40% of Louisiana state college revenues come from student tuition. If the state waived tuition, most colleges would lose millions in revenues." I drafted a Letter to the Editor expressing "Tanner Kids" support. Then I brought the letter to Superintendent Culver to sign, which he did.

Over the many years of attempts, reform efforts in Louisiana have failed due to the nature of being top down efforts. This plan, that Tanner proposed, convinced parents that their children could have reasonable chances. Change always brings benefit and loss, gain and detriment. Reform is difficult because those perceived to benefit only have a promise. Motivating people to get excited and motivated to fight for a promise is not easy. The Tanner Plan did not offer pie-in-the-sky, instead, the plan offered guarantees and hope. Something people in Louisiana could fight for.

The Tanner Plan curriculum included foreign language and math requirements as well as requiring an 18 ACT. The ACT exam would be the impartial judge of academic progress. Schools would not be able to fudge ACT scores as they could on other standardized testing attempts. The 2.5 GPA requirements would be backed-up by the ACT results. If schools are issuing inflated grades, then low ACT results would indicate their shortcomings. All schools statewide would have to offer the Tanner Plan curriculum requirements. The state would equalize academic high school offerings in order to satisfy Tanner Plan eligibility and bring many poor parishes up to modern standards for the first time.

Improved secondary education performance would reduce the need for open admissions at Louisiana's four year universities. College freshman would be expected to perform college level work which would eliminate the need for remedial classes. Funds previously used for remedial classes would be redirected to university programs. The eight regional Vo-Tech schools would become accredited Community Colleges with articulation agreements in place with the four-year universities. Students unable to satisfy university admission requirements could split enrollment between high school and a new community college and could continue academic studies earning credits transferable to a four year school or complete high school graduation requirements at a slower place while they learned a trade. Once implemented, most students would have a legitimate high school diploma and career option or heading to a state university. Tanner's offer had potential to reform Louisiana's educational system. From my perspective, a statewide Tanner plan was great because the original ideas were mine and Dean Barrilleaux's. Paul Tanner was enjoying his new status as a celebrity. And, I, a mere Creole from the 9th Ward, a kid working for coins on the street since 12 years old, the first generation of my family to receive an education, was going to Tulane University.

45

DURING THIS TIME, I had dinner with Superintendent Culver at Dave Levet's restaurant in Bay Saint Louis to explain the Plan. In addition, I called the Governor and the Chairman of the Board of Regents and I met with community leaders explaining the Tanner Plan. All politicians understand money and it made quite an impression when I arrived at small rural Louisiana airports in a Kingair 300 with PT "Papa Tango" on the tail. Most politicians were afraid of Tanner's money and his ambition and were smart enough not to oppose him … or me.

The success of a Tanner Plan depended on the success of Tanner Kids from Livingston Middle school. Job Training Partnership Act (JTPA) personnel and I planned summer study programs on local military bases and on the campuses of University of New Orleans and Loyola University New Orleans. JTPA was a federal program designed to create jobs. We also hired tutors for evening studies and used JTPA funds for the summer programs. Paul paid for field trips, special programs with celebrity speakers, and other events including a trip to his Foxworth Mississippi Ranch. We covered up allegations of rape involving four Tanner Kids on Loyola's campus and the alleged misappropriations of funds.

Marie Collins foolishly hired her sons to direct the JTPA summer programs. These programs included a job training component in addition to the academic work. The kids received small salaries for entry level jobs they filled on the college campuses. Local JTPA officials claimed that Marie's sons were misappropriating these dollars for their own use. The issue was settled after a series of private meetings in the Tanner office.

Tulane's McAlister Auditorium was the location for a motivational presentation by Montel Williams and Drew Green. This was long before Montel had his nationwide TV show. The Tanner Kids arrived on tour buses; some had never been on a tour bus or on Tulane's campus. Drew Green was a Navy pilot and Montel was a Naval Intelligence Officer. Montel, dressed in his Navy Officer dress uniform, walked across the stage, introduced himself and began speaking Chinese, pulled out a hundred dollar bill and asked, "Who was the US president at the beginning of WWII?" The Tanner kids had never seen a black man in a naval officer's uniform or heard Chinese. They thought it was a trick. After several minutes, one Tanner Kid finally got the correct answer, "Franklin Roosevelt!" Montel invited the kid on the stage and handed him the $100, explaining that he got paid for something he knows, not because he painted a house or cut grass. "That's what college can do for you." He told the audience. "You make money with your brain, not your hands."

When the Tanner staff traveled, we all wore dark suits with the same Tanner Energy tie and gold Tanner "T" lapel pin. Our ties were dark blue with numerous small yellow "T's". "You kids think you are cool." Montel continued. "You have gangs, hang around on corners smoke dope acting stupid," Montel said. "Look around. See these men in the dark suits, blue ties and gold pins? They're in a gang! They're in a gang producing oil and gas. They're in a gang that's making real money doing important stuff." He explained that there are other types of "good" gangs. "The initiation for these gangs is a college education," he said.

The lights dimmed and Rap music played over the public address system. Drew Green walked towards the stage from the back of the auditorium in the spotlight wearing a combat flight suit with dark sunglasses. "You kids think you're bad? Hanging around doing nothing acting tough." He removed the sunglasses. "I'm bad! I fly 600 miles an hour 300 feet above the ground and I can take out the whole neighborhood!"

He told them that when he entered flight training for the first time he looked at a cockpit and wondered how would he ever learn to use and understand all the gauges, controls and instruments? He told them that he studied one thing at a time and before long he was able to fly a jet fighter. "Education is like that also. Intimidating at first, but don't quit. It gets easier if you make the effort," he said.

Paul was featured in national magazines and national talk shows. One day at work, Paul Tanner said to me, "Andre, we have a TV show to do at lunch. By the way, it's in Pittsburgh." We drove to Million-Air, the Falcon Jet was ready and we took off. After the noon talk show taping, we drove back to the Pittsburgh airport and stopped at an ethnic food store where I picked up a 16-inch salami as a gift for Angela. I arrived back home at the usual time.

"Where did you get that salami, Andre?" she asked.

"Pittsburgh."

46

SUPERINTENDENT CULVER, BESE EXECUTIVE DIRECTOR Alice Therriot and the BESE staff organized a "private" Board retreat and "Team Building" conference similar to those offered by Fortune 500 corporations. Manning, Louisiana is a small resort town near Toledo Bend and Lake Sabine along the Texas-Louisiana border. Its hotel sits across the highway from Hodges Garden, which is similar to Bellingrath Gardens in Mobile, Alabama or Long Vue in New Orleans. The Gardens host an Easter Sunday service that has become a Louisiana tradition. Hodges Garden is the most beautiful and peaceful place to be on Easter Sunday morning at sunrise, but this was not Easter. Additionally, some of the best fishing in the country can be found nearby at Toledo Bend. At this time of year BESE, the staff, some reporters and lobbyist tag-alongs had the place to ourselves.

BESE member, Loselle's husband "Mose," offered to buy bait and rent poles for an afternoon fishing trip. Meetings and activities caused the day's agenda to run longer than expected and BESE members were not available until after dark. I spent the lengthy day reading the *World Economist* magazine, preferring to read *Road and Driver* but I wanted to look smarter. Although the time was late, Mose insisted on going fishing. He smiled as he opened the cheap plastic ice chest partially exposing two glass jugs labeled with a permanent marker and misspelled, "Wiskey." Mose was very proud of finding homebrew in a dry parish. We climbed into his 1977 Cadillac Deville and headed out to the dam at Lake Sabine and Toledo Bend, a thirty-minute drive.

John Honoree declared the whiskey to be of "high quality" and passed the jug around and around. Soon Bankston was complaining about things crawling on the floor. "Stop the car! Stop the car!" Keith was frantically removing his pants while Carson was trying to climb into the front seat. "Turn on the fucking lights. There's something back here." As Mose stopped the car, the back seat emptied like a fire drill. Keith fell to the ground tripped up by his half-off pants. Upon entering the car, someone kicked over a half-gallon ice cream container filled with live crickets, purchased for bait. Fishing was now out of the question, but we proceeded to the dam anyhow.

Stopping a short drive out along the dam we sat on the rocks; finished off the first whiskey jug and got a good start on the second. Keith tried to throw the empty jug into the lake, but it fell well short and shattered near Wilmer. He did not seem to notice and continued to stare at the stars and asked, "How long is this dam?" Mose had the doors of the Cadillac open as he worked to round up the remaining crickets. The rest of us discussed foreign policy and Department of Education secretaries' asses.

Wilmer walked towards Mose and demanded that he close the Cadillac doors. "Give me the keys." He started the engine and turned the car around. We covered our faces as Wilmer sped away spraying gravel with the tires squealing and the backend fishtailing like a Redfish. Mose gave chase on foot for a short distance, walked back, and asked for the whiskey.

"Fuck it," he said. The Cadillac's taillights grew dim as Wilmer reached the Louisiana side of the dam and disappeared from view.

We were content to sit and finish the second whiskey jug when we heard the roar of the Cadillac V8 again. This time we saw headlights screaming towards us. "Get in! Get in!" Wilmer demanded. We all climbed back in. Carson was reluctant because Wilmer had been drinking and he was heading in the wrong direction anyhow, "towards Houston!" said Carson.

"What are you going to do? Walk home?" Keith asked. Carson headed off in the opposite direction on foot.

The earthen dam is long with the Texas-Louisiana state line somewhere in the middle. We drove for a certain distance with Wilmer's eyes locked on the odometer. He hit the brakes hard. "OK, everybody out." He shut off the engine and handed the keys back to Mose. Wilmer had calculated distance and stopped the car once we were over the state line on the Texas side, "no longer in Louisiana." He thought it would look bad if we were arrested for drinking in a dry parish. Keith and I walked back and found Carson sleeping face down in the road. Two of us got on either side of Carson, put our arms under his shoulders, and hauled him all the way to Texas. He did not wake up as his feet dragged behind. Carson still wonders how he got holes on the tops of his Bostonian wingtips.

47

MY COMMITMENTS TO PAUL TANNER were full time, sometimes as much as 60 hours per week. After the office closed, we usually had drinks. I was beginning to worry about the heavy alcohol consumption and began drinking only tonic whenever possible. Often we would decide to go out for dinner at the last minute. Paul did not want to go home to Mrs. Tanner and expected employees to accept his last minute late night invitations. He had fired people for less. As an example, each year Tanner Energy employees participated in the March of Dimes walkathon. Nora sent a discrete memo reminding everyone to stay behind Paul. A secretary disregarded the notice and walked at the head of the group. Paul said that her ass looked like "two puppies in a sack." He fired her.

Mr. Tanner was always quick on the trigger when firing employees. The Lee Circle building has a balcony overlooking St. Charles Avenue along one of the Mardi Gras parade routes. A secretary brought her teenage son and his girlfriend to view the parade. The girlfriend raised her shirt to get more beads thrown her way, a New Orleans tradition On Monday morning Paul fired the secretary when she refused to apologize.

A Tanner Energy drilling platform in the Gulf of Mexico south of Lake Charles spilled a quantity of drilling mud into Gulf waters. Environmental Protection Agency fines and investigations ensued. Paul asked Congressman Lynchard to "fix" things. Lynchard refused.

Paul reminded me that he would spend whatever was necessary to defeat that ingrate when the time came. From his point of view, loyalty was only a one-way street, especially when he thought he already bought and paid for someone. Don't ever cross Paul Tanner!

At 7:00 PM one evening, Paul decided we should go out for Greek food. The car was waiting, but traffic this evening was unusually heavy. Paul instructed the chauffer to drive on the neutral ground along the streetcar tracks, bypassing the backed-up traffic. Obviously, this created an unusual sight even in New Orleans for a Mercedes sedan driving on the neutral ground dodging streetcars. Arriving at the restaurant Paul waited with one bodyguard while another checked-out the dining room.

Traffic was blocked intentionally to prevent unknown cars from pulling alongside the Tanner vehicles. A young driver behind us became impatient, horn blowing, engine racing, waving his hands, and flashing obscene jesters. "Dumb move," I thought and watched as the menacing figure of Paul's security approach the irate driver. "What the fuck is wrong with you people? You can't block the whole damn street!" I could not hear the entire dialog but did see Dennis casually opened his jacket exposing his many weapons. Dennis soon returned and the short tempered driver decided to relax and wait quietly. I guess he decided it was not worth it.

Working for Paul was always demanding and BESE time commitments had grown to be open-ended. Each night I had phone calls to return usually from people adversely affected by the impending statewide Reduction In Force (RIF) plans. Further, in an effort to complete the Tulane Degree as quickly as possible, I was taking night classes, Saturday classes, and some sunrise classes. After two semesters, I had 24 earned credits. Tulane was a top priority as I did not know when, or if, Mr. Tanner would change his mind regarding the tuition. I felt my position was secure as long as Tanner stayed interested in education reform and his hatred for Congressman Lynchard persisted. I drank coffee with chicory all day long and drove to a Slidell truck stop regularly to buy bottles of No-Doze pills that I ate like candy.

48

MUCH OF THE HUMAN EXPERIENCE takes place in school buildings. Each room filled with its own set of unique memories, the smell of plaster walls, the ambience of a school lunch room or the voice of a favorite teacher. In an old school building, we are reminded that each generation must yield to the next, including our own. Closing any school is a difficult and heart wrenching experience. However, as demographics shift change dictated by economics is often necessary. Louisiana was facing a budget crisis and losing significant population at the same time. School consolidation saves money by reducing fixed costs. Consolidated schools require only one principal, one janitorial service, one lunch room, less maintenance and so on; costs reductions are significant. The business decision to close schools is often recommended by accountants, while the true impact of consolidation is borne by communities who feel they are losing part of their identity.

The difficult decisions to consolidate Vo-Tech schools rested upon my inexperienced shoulders. The Superintendent asked BESE to call an emergency Saturday meeting to discuss the deepening budget crises. All programs would be affected with the most severe cuts falling upon the Vocational Education system as that funding was unprotected. The Superintendent also expected BESE to make voluntary across-the-board cuts affecting nearly all other programs in the 66 school systems including the Louisiana School for the Deaf, School for the Visually Impaired, The Louisiana School for Math and

Science, and the state Special Education Centers. "We all need to do our part to help the state at this difficult time," Keith said. However, his plan protected the interest of New Orleans at the expense of everyone else. Vo-Tech education in New Orleans had been corrupted by political groups long ago. Keith was trying to protect political patronage, not economic development or educational opportunity.

"What cuts have the Department of Natural Resources made, what about the Department of Insurance or Labor what about that fleet of state owned airplanes?" Carson asked while waving his arms mimicking an airplane while pretending to glide around the room. "Our job is to protect education not destroy it." Carson made a motion that "BESE do nothing at this time and take the Superintendent's information under advisement."

Keith tried to block Killen by declaring "order of the day," a parliamentary maneuver designed to hijack the agenda. Carson explained that "across the board" cuts are the politicians' ways of protecting their ass by avoiding difficult decisions. "It throws out the "baby with the bath water," according to Carson.

The impact from the proposed cuts to the Vo-Tech system would result in the closure of 21 schools. Some of these schools were satellites of larger campuses, but most were successful well attended programs in operation for decades. In many rural Louisiana towns, Vo-Tech schools were the only postsecondary education and job training available. In the Houma-Thibodaux area, the Marine Institute trained workers for jobs in the oil patch. Closing that particular school would be a vote of no-confidence in Louisiana's most important industry and encourage the exodus of petroleum jobs to Houston.

A meeting was organized in New Orleans at the Heritage Plaza office tower to discuss the proposed closure attended by representatives from many of the major oil and gas exploration companies. The Superintendent's spokesman claimed that the across-the-board cuts were the only way to keep the state's fiscal head above water. Earlier that day, the credit rating agencies (S&P, Fitch) placed Louisiana debt on negative outlook meaning a rating cut is more likely than an upgrade and indicates a possible downgrade to junk status – the lowest rating. The Superintendent's spokesman explained that "hands are tied" in this unfortunate matter and actions were dictated by sound fiscal responsibility. Many of the proposed school closures were in John Honoree's district, because that area depended heavily on oil patch job training. "I can't be lied to! I can't be lied to!" John repeated as he aggressively moved towards the frightened spokesman.

"Settle down old John," Carson said without looking up. "It's only a proposal."

The Vo-Tech school directors organized a rally on the capital steps in support of vocational training. The protest was planned on a day when both the legislature and BESE were in session. News reports placed the attendance at over ten thousand, buses blocked traffic around the capital. State Senators and Representatives entered the building by a side door to avoid confrontations with the angry blue collar protest. As chairman of the Vo-Tech governing committee I was the first to address the crowd. "I do not intend to preside over the dismantling of vocational education."

Later that day, I received a call from the Governor. "Andre, regular people in Louisiana are never going to attend Harvard. The best most will ever do is job training at the local Vo-Tech. If you take that away they have nothing. Those people you saw on the steps of the Capital today are my people."

I pointed out the budget problems. "It is not a question of funding; it is a question of political agendas and priorities." I asked the Governor what options I had.

"Well, the way I see it, Andre, you have only two options. You can give them back their money or you can kill them all," he said.

"Governor I can't kill ten thousand people"

Then he said "give them back their money!"

I asked the Governor and BESE to consider establishing a "Blue Ribbon" commission to study vocational education and establish a plan for growth, relevance and its place as a legitimate postsecondary offering. This proposal gave everyone political cover while the state continued to define budget needs and school closings would postponed while the panel worked. Everything was open for discussion including, turning some schools over to a private corporation, creating the community college system, creating a new governing board, stiffer regulation, oversight of private training schools, and accreditation. The chairman also acknowledged that establishing a new community college system supporting a Tanner Plan program would be on the agenda for discussion.

BESE staff was unable to provide information requested by the study commission because the data did not exist. I asked, "How many students were enrolled in Vo-Tech schools state-wide, how many students obtained jobs, how many dropped out before completing a program, did quick start programs ever attract new industry, how much money is spent on each program?" In the early 1980's mainframe computers were purchased for each of the eight regional Vo-Tech schools. Each region was then expected to report to BESE and the Department of Education. Funding was cut before the mainframe system was operational and thereafter the computers were used primarily to track student grades and teacher schedules, nothing more.

Without adequate data, the Committee was limited to making recommendations using only anecdotal stories provided during closed door testimony like using quick start funds to train Licensed Practicing Nurses at existing hospitals or using automobile technology programs to repair employee's cars. According to sworn testimony, in Baton Rouge, a complete restoration was allegedly done on a 1968 International Scout for a lobbyist, in Slidell a home was built on the director's property using the school resources and a state senator kept his horse on the grounds of a Vo-Tech school in central Louisiana,. If the panel could not reach conclusions, then how could BESE close schools when it was nearly impossible to measure outcomes in any meaningful way? The incompetence and inertia of the system saved it from the budget ax until better management came along.

49

THE VOCATIONAL EDUCATION CHAIRMANSHIP WAS becoming a curse. I wanted an experienced College Administrator to run the New Orleans Regional Vocational Education Center and work to qualify the school for accreditation. Accreditation would allow the articulation of Vo-Tech credits towards admission at Louisiana's four-year universities and two-year colleges. The New Orleans Regional Vo-Tech is located on the north side of Delgado's campus, but unlike its successful neighbor, never offered worthwhile training. A qualified director with solid academic credentials could more easily make the case for establishing a statewide community college system.

The previous director of the New Orleans school was transferred to a Jefferson Parish Vo-Tech and Simone Senac was named as acting director. The Department of Education began the hiring process by advertising for the permanent position and reviewing applications. Those not meeting the minimum requirements would be weeded out, the remaining candidates would be interviewed by Superintendent Culver's staff and referred to BESE for a final review. However, the window to apply for the open position was unexpectedly and suspiciously cut short eliminating most qualified candidates.

My motion to extend the application time period reopening the process was approved by a thin margin of 6-5. The BESE president only votes in the event of a tie. Alice Therriot walked over to Keith's chair and whispered instructions in his ear. Keith excused himself from the meeting and following protocol temporarily relinquishing the chair to vice president John Honoree. A motion to reconsider can only be brought by the prevailing side. Keith had not voted therefore was technically eligible to reintroduce the motion. With a confused and fumbling Honoree as acting president, Keith called for a revote and voted against the motion. As Honoree was now 'temporary president' and unable to vote, the decision went 6-5 in the other direction, qualifying was not reopened. The acting director, Simone Senac, was named permanent director.

I walked to the rear of the auditorium and sat down next to a disinterested looking newspaper reporter from New Orleans. "Do you realize who Simone Senac is?" I asked.

"Some department bureaucrat I guess. Why do you ask, Andree?"

"She is the wife of Louis Senac the city's chief legislative lobbyist working for the New Orleans Mayor. Louis Senac, her husband, is also a former New Orleans legislator." I explained that Keith works for the city in the Department of Safety and Permits. "Do you think that is all coincidence?" I walked away as the reporter opened a small notebook and began writing.

"BESE should take another vote and vote to follow a proper search procedure to find a new director whose hiring it can justify to the public on sound professional and educational grounds," according to the news articles. The paper followed with three prominent stories and an editorial page opinion blasting the Simone hire and calling vocational education a "patronage playground."

Keith said, "The school's students will be better served with a connection to the Legislature, which approves funding, than with any pointy headed community college instructor."

50

KEITH NEVER GAVE UP AND planned to use the redistricting process to remove the New Orleans Regional school from my control altogether. Every ten years Louisiana redraws political maps based on new census numbers. Unpopular politicians have been yanked out of safe districts and placed in new districts with unbeatable incumbents, ending political careers. The party that controls the state house and senate also selects the committee chair that guides the redistricting process. Losing the redistricting battle can condemn a party to second class status for a decade; winning can make it unbeatable. Senator Hamill said "redistricting crippled more people than polio." However, Hamill benefited more than most. His senatorial district stretched from his Victorian home in uptown New Orleans across the conservative areas of Jefferson Parish, and over the center of Lake Pontchartrain to Mandeville in St. Tammany Parish where he had a lakefront home. The gerrymander district was made contiguous by the 24-mile Causeway that connects both sides of the lake.

Redistricting is also used to wield political control over hospitals, universities, bridges, stadiums, roads or any other government enterprise that spends money and creates jobs, giving politicians the opportunity to carve Louisiana up like a ripe melon. In the New Orleans Regional case, the state legislature was expected to support the redistricting plan favored by the majority of BESE members. Keith traveled the state and met with each BESE member individually offering a deal. "If we stick together nobody gets hurt," he said. His plan would leave the other seven districts nearly unchanged with one exception. Keith's 2nd District would finger across City Park into the 1st District and pick up the New Orleans Regional Vo-Tech Institute, cut me out of any activity involving the school, sabotage the community college expansion effort, and protect Simone Senac as Director. The other BESE members were quick to sacrifice me if it meant protecting their own interest; my district was carved up.

The hearing in Committee Room 1 of the Capital Building was standing room only with politicians and lobbyist juggling for position as many redistricting issues were on the agenda. Labor, business and industry, education, timber, and construction, all had a vested interest in the outcome. Most politicians responded positively to my request for assistance because they were afraid of Paul Tanner's wrath. Paul wanted a community college system and he wanted a Tanner Plan for college availability, and politicians always want money. When they asked Paul for contributions, it was always in person, face to face as he would not respond to mail or phone request.

"That is a great idea. I would love to support your candidacy," he would say from behind his desk. The "hat in hand" politician sat on a leather chair directly in front of Paul's desk. Paul had the legs of the chair cut slightly uneven so that he looked down upon his off balance guests. I usually sat in a chair to Paul's left.

Paul Tanner studied the backgrounds of elected officials and used that information in interesting ways. He drank when he met Bible thumpers from North Louisiana and had an exceptionally good looking secretary interrupt meetings with so called, "family men." He hung an oil portrait of Robert E. Lee for other occasions. He had someone go out and take pictures of the politician's car. "How someone takes care of their car says a lot about character," he said. The righteous always accepted a drink and the others kept their eyes focused on Candy's large breasts and erect nipples. Many did both. Paul would make them uncomfortable, then sat back and study their reactions, looking for weakness and faults. His assistant was trained to interrupt on cue. Whispering just loud enough in an urgent tone to be overheard, "Mr. Tanner, the president is holding."

I enjoyed watching the various reactions to this intimidating and uncomfortable setup. A young state representative from New Orleans East was discreetly rubbing himself while mesmerized by Candy's nipples, which resembled the erasers on fat preschool pencils. Paul gave him nothing. According to Ebony American magazine, he was one of the top "up and coming" black men in the country. This Representative also enjoyed ordering room service and striping down to nothing before inviting the bellhops into his room. He was arrested in a Baton Rouge hotel and claimed it was all the result of a political vendetta against powerful black men. Paul was not at all surprised. "I told you so," he said.

"I would love to support your election, but Andre reviews all these requests for me. Call him next week." After the meetings, Paul would either write a check or decide to give nothing. When he gave nothing, he blamed me and apologized claiming that I could be stingy and hardheaded. Soon, I had the reputation of controlling the largest political war chest in Louisiana. Clearly, this reputation was an inaccurate perception because Paul made all his own decisions, but it was politically useful to me nevertheless. The Representatives I called were falling over themselves to keep the Orleans Regional Vo-Tech in the 1st District where Mr. Tanner wanted it.

"Make sure you tell Mr. Paul how helpful I have been," was the usual response.

Keith confidently walked over to the wall where the proposed maps were posted. He saw Districts with minor adjustments as proposed and he was pleased. Then he reached the 1st and 2nd BESE District maps and realized that the Regional School was placed back in the 1st. Just to piss him off more, Kennedy High School, one of the city's largest public schools and located on the eastern edge of City Park, was moved out of the 2nd and into the 1st. District.

"I don't have much interest in keeping Kennedy in the 1st. However the New Orleans Regional will stay put. That is non negotiable," I explained to Keith. "I also expect your support for the Tanner Plan at the BESE and Regents meeting next month."

Realizing he was beat he offered a fishy handshake and a disgusted look. "What the fuck!" he said.

The final redistricting maps placed the New Orleans Regional in the 1st District and moved Kennedy High School back to the 2nd District, as promised. The bill was approved by both houses and signed by the Governor. Keith took nothing personal. This issue was done; we moved on with the knowledge that we would most likely need each other in the future. "*Le temps marche*," as they say in New Orleans, time marches on.

51

THE LOUISIANA CONSTITUTION REQUIRED AN annual meeting between BESE and the Board of Regents. BESE is the most powerful elementary and secondary board and the Board of Regents, the top College Board. The location alternated between the two facilities. I always enjoyed meeting at the Regent's office because it was a beautifully restored historic bank building with polished marble and granite, a pleasant change from the rundown BESE complex. Nothing much ever developed from these meetings except for the occasional enthusiastic trading of LSU football tickets. However, this time would be different; I placed an item on this agenda calling for the consideration of the Tanner Plan concept. I considered this meeting a perfect venue because the Tanner Plan would directly impact both elementary and postsecondary education state-wide.

Since this meeting was at the Regent's office, their president would be the presiding officer, leaving Keith free to make the motion supporting the Tanner Plan, as he promised to do. I would offer the second. Greg O'Leary, Chancellor of the University of New Orleans, was present to support the Plan. O'Leary looked at me oddly, but I do not think he ever made the connection with the Mondale Campaign VW episode years before when I was the College Republican President.

Paul funded a program providing free laptop computers, a semi-annual $2,000 cash stipend, and tuition waiver for any National Merit Finalist or Semifinalist attending UNO. Eventually seventeen students accepted the offer that first year. The Merit scholarship program was especially impressive considering that UNO is consistently ranked as mediocre by US World Report's annual survey of American Colleges and Universities. National Merit winners can go anywhere. The fact that some National Merit winners selected UNO was a testament to the powerful need for college financial availability. The program became controversial when O'Leary's daughter, an average student, somehow received the benefits of Paul's Merit Scholarship offer.

The Regents facilities were decorated for Christmas and we all enjoyed cookies and hot buttered rum before the meeting. Keith and I presented the mechanics of the plan and solicited the support of individual Regents explaining that we wanted a vote supporting the concept at this time. The Regents saw Paul's plan as a lucrative new source of funding and more qualified students for higher education. A favorable vote here would also give us the ability to enlist the full resources of the State Department of Education including the Superintendent's office once a Tanner Plan Bill was introduced in the legislature.

The joint meeting was called to order. Our item was second on a short agenda. Keith made the motion supporting the Tanner Plan for College Availability in concept and I offered the second. Dr. O'Leary offered personal accounts of commitment and additional supporting testimony. Others explained the positive impact on the Community College system and O'Leary explained the importance of university freshmen entering prepared for college level work. "The plan could force improvements at the secondary level allowing admission requirements at Louisiana Universities for the first time," O'Leary said. The necessary votes were already lined up, but members wanted their support recorded in the record as they knew Paul would study the meeting minutes. The question was called and the motion carried unanimously.

The single reporter in attendance called in his "Tanner Plan" story that was quickly picked up by the Associated Press and carried statewide. Paul called, "Nice job. Stay where you are. Don't leave," were his instructions. Soon his Mercedes limousine arrived to take me back to New Orleans. This was also the night of the Tanner's Christmas party at the Fairmont Grand Ballroom, the biggest bash of the holiday season on the New Orleans calendar and Paul had much to celebrate. The Mercedes was mine for the night and I looked forward to picking up Angela and enjoying what promised to be a memorable celebration.

On the center of the dance floor was a fifteen foot tall Christmas tree made entirely of red and yellow poinsettias. Hundreds of golden ornaments hung from the tree intended as party favors. The orchestra played holiday favorites and the lines at the four bars were long as the party got started. The displays of Louisiana boiled seafood were irresistible and roasted pigs were carved nearby with great pageantry. Three double stainless steel doors at the back wall opened at once and numerous servers in formal black tails emerged with trays of crab cakes, bacon wrapped shrimp and crab claws. Paul stood with Mrs. Tanner at his side, thanked everyone for their support as he recounted the day's success at the Regent's meeting. Mr. and Mrs. Tanner were always the perfect elegant couple in public and Mrs. Tanner was especially beautiful this night. Paul recognized the many political and educational leaders in attendance, an imperial evening celebrating wealth and power with Louisiana's most beautiful people.

I made my way through the adoring crowds to shake his hand. "You did well today! How was the limo? If I had access to a car like that at your age I would have been fucking all day long. Hope you enjoyed yourself" he said. "Keep it up Andre. The perks can only get better."

An engineer for the Tanner Energy Company made his way over to my table, but did not sit down. "Since you have been around, Paul has little interest in running the company. He seldom takes my call and seems disinterested. The last two holes we drilled were dry. He doesn't care." People say stupid things when drinking, he didn't stop. "Did you know that NBC Bank has asked Paul to resign from their board, because our company is delinquent on loan obligations? Tanner is an egomaniacal, self-promoting braggadocios fool. When will he realize that all this political foolishness is a serious business distraction?"

I asked another employee to drive him home before he got himself in real trouble. "All this foolishness that you call a business distraction is Paul's business!" I said as he was escorted out. I took Angela's hand and we headed for the dance floor.

52

BEFORE IMPLEMENTATION OF TANNER PLAN legislation into law, a funding mechanism had to be identified. The cost of setting up the program was an estimated $1,900,000 to $2,500,000 according to the Governor's Budget Office. Tuition waivers could cost many millions more. Conveniently, BESE had long been criticized for the way it handled the $25,000,000 to $35,000,000 annual 8g educational trust fund dollars received. 8g represents Louisiana's share of mineral revenue from the first three miles of federal land in the Gulf of Mexico. 8g represented an ideal funding source for the Tanner Plan.

The inept Elementary and Secondary funding plan for 8g dollars was spread over many small projects. Critics said funding should have been focused on major problems rather than the shotgun approach employed by BESE. Some funds were used to pay BESE member travel expenses, buy expensive sole source software, or wasted on useless hardware. One segment of 8g funding implemented by BESE was fraudulent by design. This funding plan became perhaps the most blatant theft of public funds perpetrated by an elected body upon Louisiana taxpayers in modern memory.

This allocation scheme left millions available for graft and corruption executed through a separate noncompetitive exemplarity grant program. The noncompetitive 8g funding program was disguised to reward creative thinking and give smaller school systems an equal opportunity to win funding awards. Each year, BESE established a new list of eligible categories that was advertised statewide and RFP's (requests for proposals) were then issued to School Boards, Vo-Techs and Special Schools. Once submitted the proposals were reviewed by staff for eligibility criteria then divided into the specific categories.

Grants were funded based on review and scoring by appointed readers. Each BESE member appointed three readers whose task it was to score proposals individually. The readers received blind copies identifiable only by a code and scored them on a 1-100 point scale. Every individual proposal was reviewed three times by three different readers.

BESE staff members compiled the reader's individual scores on each proposal and determined an average. The final score was the average of three. Funding was awarded in each category, highest scoring proposals first and then down the point list until the money ran out. However, the lowest and highest scores for each review were not thrown out as a reasonable person might expect. Accountability was not a priority as "strict accountability and outcome expectations would stifle creativity," according to Keith.

My instructions were clear. At the appointed time, drive to a certain parking lot adjacent to a local Baton Rouge Chinese restaurant turn off my headlights, but keep the motor running. I was not going to just a meeting at a café for a cup of coffee. The Investigative Reporter said he was working on an explosive investigative story involving the 8g program and needed to, "Fill in a few holes." I had been waiting only a few minutes, when I noticed a gold Volvo station wagon pulling into the parking area. Heading in my direction, the car's high beams flashed twice. I turned on my lights and pulled into traffic behind the Volvo.

I followed the reporter on a confusing route through Baton Rouge residential neighborhoods. After fifteen minutes of driving, I pulled over to the side of the road and opened the car's hood as I had been instructed. The reporter would circle back and check for anyone who might have followed us. For nearly one half hour, we doubled back and circled around until finally pulling into a long brick driveway across the lake from LSU's Sorority Row, not far from where we started. I thought how silly all these theatrics were, but also wondered if I was in a real den of snakes and maybe did not recognize the serious nature of the danger involved. What did the reporter know that I did not? Two garage doors opened and closed quickly as soon as both cars entered.

"I apologize for the OO7 stuff, but you can't be too careful. Please realize that was all done for your protection. What we discuss tonight will be off the record. No one will know of this meeting except you and me," he said as we shook hands and headed into the house directly from the garage. The home was expensive and upscale and probably did not belong to the reporter. The floors were made of eight inch oak planks rescued from a century old New Orleans riverfront warehouse. They were polished to a reflective shine but not refinished and bore the scars sustained during their previous life like a badge of honor. The home contained no personal items that would give a hint to its ownership. We sat on leather chairs and began with discussions of Perestroika and Glasnost as well as other changes taking place in Russia at that time, before turning to BESE issues.

"Please explain the real inside process used by BESE to allocate the 8g funds," he asked. "What do you know about this unusual Adult Education grant in East Baton Rouge Parish? What about this push to offer Writing and Reading software statewide? Who benefits financially from that?" I felt I was receiving an interrogation without the bright light and almost expected to be hit in the back of the head with a phonebook. I tried to answer his questions as thoroughly as possible. "I have two eye witness accounts claiming the Board President Keith Hayes recently removed from a department office two televisions and other equipment purchased with 8g funds." Keith denied the accusation and I had no personal knowledge of the incident. An internal review turned up nothing new. The reporter intended to expose Keith as a thief and wanted my collaboration of his version of events. I was unable to provide any useful information.

The reporter was not even close to the real issues of fraud and corruption I had expected to discuss. Exposing the shocking 8g truth would have made this reporter's career like Woodward and Bernstein; instead he was chasing politically motivated stories about petty theft. Keith may have helped himself to taxpayer provided equipment but that was of little long-term consequence. I did not volunteer any new information at all and only answered the specific questions asked.

53

IN ORDER TO TAKE ADVANTAGE of 8g noncompetitive grants, Keith and NWAC formed a secret partnership with a testing and educational products company called Quest Education Inc. headquartered in Pineville, a small community near Alexandria. Quest operated with a limited full-time staff on a campus of three doublewide trailers converted to fit their unique needs. The corporate headquarters was maintained nearby in a small structure with a TV with rabbit ears sitting on a folding metal stand and an electric Lazy-e-Boy recliner with a built-in back massager as its only furnishings. Before meeting Keith, the company's only business were local distribution rights for rubberized foam puzzles and floor mats gaining widespread use in early education programs around the country. With Keith's influence peddling and skullduggery skills, this tiny company would make some BESE members wealthy and become the most successful 8g noncompetitive grant recipient ever with an unprecedented record of funding mischief. Yet, their name did not appear in BESE reports or state archives.

Quest's expertise designing 8g grant proposals for Special Education and Vocational Education programs involving overpriced hardware and expensive sole-source software was perfected over a period of time. A group of well written applications could be modified as needed to fit individual submission criteria and create the illusion of uniqueness. Each individual proposal was titled and identified by the school or ghost writer making the submission and never under the Quest name. The company coerced and bribed school directors and administrative personal to submit the Quest designed proposals; many received a piece of the action for their trouble. Once a school official accepted cash; they were considered trustworthy.

Those displaying ethical scruples were looked upon with suspicion, others played along because they feared retribution. Ten to twenty Quest grant requests were submitted from school districts and Vo-Tech schools each year. Once the proposals cleared the initial eligibility review by BESE staff, identifying characteristics and information were removed, then each was assigned a coded tracking number. The tracking number master list was locked away in the Director's office. All eligible grant proposals were then distributed at random to the readers appointed by all BESE members.

Quest could identify their proposals by unique imbedded language, coded type or unique software descriptions. The corrupted BESE readers then assigned scores of 98-100 on the Quest proposals. All other non-Quest proposals received scores less than 10, knocking them out of consideration. Keith also worked to convince other BESE members to influence their readers by promising to deliver high scores for hometown proposals or pet projects. Numerous winning slots on the funding lists were assured. High profitability was designed into each grant allowing lucrative compensation for the conspirators involved. The real losers in this 8g misadventure were the dedicated educators whose legitimate proposals were crowded out and denied fair consideration. Quality educators spent years perfecting worthy proposals that never had a chance.

Simply telling Keith that I knew how this scheme worked was not hardball enough to get and hold his attention. He called the regular BESE meeting to order and I requested a point of personal privilege. This parliamentary maneuver allowed a member to address the meeting before official business began. This procedure was used primarily to introduce visitors from a home district, award winners or other dignitaries. I had other ideas.

Items for consideration were first placed on the agenda for referral to the appropriate committee. After committee deliberations concluded the item would be placed on the agenda for final consideration by the full board the next meeting. The process could take months, but I planned a short cut. "Mr. President, may I have a point of personal privilege?" I asked while other members chatted amongst themselves or with constituents and drank coffee. "The recent criticism we have received in the press regarding 8g funding has created a window of opportunity for us to make some important and overdue changes. First, I propose a new spending plan that will bar use of this money for member's travel expenses."

BESE members received reimbursement for travel and entertainment expenses from 8g dollars as other available funding sources were eliminated by budget shortfalls. "This new plan will direct spending to a few of the state's most severe problems and educational needs and abolish the practice of spreading the appropriations among too many small noncompetitive projects that yield little significant return." I had everyone's attention especially Keith. "Half of the annual funds will be dedicated to addressing the dropout problem and early education programs. The other half will be used to finance the administration and implementation of the Tanner Plan," I said.

"He is out of line!" John Honoree screamed from the other end of the table. "I demand that you call him out of order! Mr. President do your job!"

"Mr. Dupree has the floor for personal privilege," Keith said in a very calm voice. I continued to read the statement as John continued to interrupt. The discussion was eventually dropped because the personal privilege recommendations were not intended as an agenda item for consideration. However, I managed to get Keith's attention.

That night was the annual Louisiana Teacher of the Year Banquet sponsored by the Department of Education and underwritten by the School Book Depository. At this banquet, Louisiana's best teacher is announced before a crowd of hundreds. A finalist and runner-up from each parish are invited, local school board members and administrators are also in attendance. My job, on this night, was to deliver a welcome address on behalf of BESE and the Department of Education. I carefully prepared notes and placed a printed copy on the podium before hand, it ran about three pages. I was introduced by the Superintendent, thanked him and the others in attendance and then looked down at my prepared comments. The pages were blank, Keith switched them.

54

THE NEXT WEEKEND I WAS sitting in a rocking chair on the front porch of my Slidell home early Saturday morning, reading the paper, and enjoying a cup of coffee when an enclosed flatbed truck turned into the driveway. The house sat on nearly two wooded acres with a circular drive. The large truck had trouble negotiating the turns while avoiding the fence and pine trees. My love of antique automobiles was well-known, but I was not expecting this.

The 1956 Packard Caribbean convertible finished in beautiful tuxedo black and camel and black leather and wool interior was the nicest automobile that I have seen. Options included push button Ultramatic transmission, power steering, power brakes, power windows, power seats, power antennas, signal seeking radio and dual quad carburetors atop a massive 374 cid V8. Packard was known for building spectacular engines including the Twin Six, the WWI Liberty motor, the WWII Packard-Merlin P-51 Mustang motor and PT boat engines. The Caribbean also had the remarkable Twin Traction and Torsion-Level ride systems. This car represented the last full year of production before Packard's disappearance from the American road. Only 270 Caribbean convertibles were built in 1956 as financial mismanagement caught up with Packard.

"There must be a mistake. This does not belong to me." I said as the cantankerous driver unloaded the Packard.

"I just deliver, dude, this is the address on the paperwork. You Andre Dupree? Sign here." He handed me a greasy pen that appeared to double as a Q-Tip for cleaning his wax filled ears. Wedged between the front seats was a note from Quest Education thanking me for future support of their grants to 'improve' Louisiana's schools expressing the hope that we would have a stronger relationship going forward. "The Packard is an expression of our good faith," the note read. The driver climbed back into the truck's cab, loudly passed gas that sounded like tearing fabric and then made his way back to the main road. Angela came out on the porch and sat down to read the paper. She rolled her eyes in the direction of the Packard, but asked nothing.

55

THE TANNER PLAN LEGISLATION WAS written by Gary Lee, a Department of Education employee. Senator Hamill claimed to author the bill, but this is simply not true. Hamill signed on as an early co-sponsor, offered a few minor changes, and claimed it as his own. He pointed out that "irregardless" should be "regardless," that's it. Gary was very quiet and nearly blind, but was responsible for tracking all legislation moving through the Capitol that could impact education. Once the legislature was in session, Gary's job became more important as his opinion was heavily weighted when determining Department of Education positions. Having followed and studied the Louisiana Legislature for years, he had a clear understanding of the procedures and players.

Lee had a small, but neat interior office with no windows, although the faux curtains did create an effective illusion similar to interior cabins on a cruise ship. The pile of messages on his desk read like a list of Who's Who among Louisiana's top power brokers. "I can help shepherd the Tanner legislation, but do you have any other plans for lobbying support? If not, you really should consider that," he said as he re-read the Bill from behind thick glasses. He cocked his head at an unusual angle to improve his line of vision. From across the desk, he appeared to have giant fish eyes. "Lobbyist will sell you out the minute something more lucrative comes along, they can also protect you. Their loyalty is to money and power only. Here's the reality, you can't pass anything without them," he said. "In this case you can expect amendments and objections because of who Tanner is. Every swinging dick in town will use this as an opportunity to shake him down! Promoting himself as the richest man in Louisiana doesn't help." The finished Legislation was only 1 ½ pages long. "Short, but effective," Gary said.

I took his advice. "Mr. Tanner, we will need to consider hiring a lobbyist, if we want to end up with a Tanner Plan Bill we recognize." I explained the complicated process of passing a Bill and some of the politics involved. Paul once hired an expensive Washington DC firm after the Exxon Valdez accident. He expected them to convince Congress that the Exxon accident was a transportation failure, not drilling and exploration. The effort was unsuccessful and Tanner Energy faced many new expensive environmental regulations as a result. He felt lobbyists delivered nothing for his money. "Now, we are talking about lobbyist again. They're all thieves. Do we even need a bill?" he wondered aloud. "We have Resolutions from the Education Boards and the Governor has offered to sponsor another. Why do we need legislation?"

I folded my hands together on his desk and looked into his eyes, "This process will create law! Nothing else can do that."

I contacted a lobbyist in New Orleans who had recent high profile successes representing business interest including the Chamber, Business Council and the Louisiana Association of Business. I explained our current position and he expressed initial interest. We agreed to meet at a coffee shop on Tulane's campus after my last class that evening. The meeting went poorly because by 10:00 PM I was dead tired. We began with small talk about his new Jaguar. He said it has been reliable except that he had the engine replaced. The failure was caused by a defective manufacturing issue that the dealer corrected.

We quickly got down to business, but he was upset because I had nothing in writing to offer. "Having nothing in writing tells me that you are not really serious," he said.

"Fine, but first we want to see a vita and references," I insisted. "Do you think I am some college kid applying for his first job?" If I had insisted on seeing a resume I would have discovered his RDA and Frank Bradley affiliation. I liked his spunk and I set up a meeting the following week with Paul. The $7,500 per month annual retainer was outrageous, but Paul signed the contract. Unknown to me, Frank Bradley would be involved as part of the deal.

56

IN AN EFFORT TO RECOGNIZE Paul Tanner's efforts, First Lady Barbara Bush planned a New Orleans visit. While in the city she asked to meet the Tanner Kids. The national press coverage of the First Lady speaking with them created world wide exposure. President George H.W. Bush was eager to show a compassionate side of the Republican Party and a rich conservative "Oil Man" helping inner city black children was perfect public relations. Mrs. Bush had called the Tanner Energy office several times that I am aware of and displayed a sincere interest in the children. In a Washington receiving line for Republican Eagles, she turned to her husband and said "Look George, here are our friends from Louisiana" as Paul and Mrs. Tanner were presented.

As a result of the White House publicity, Hour One News with Walter Wallace suggested a segment on the Tanner Kids and Tanner Plan legislation. As an "Oil Man," Paul had many unpleasant encounters with the media and was inclined to say no thanks. "You know it is going to be a bad day when you wake up and see Walter Wallace standing on your front lawn." Paul liked to say. The network assured us that this was to be a human interest story not an investigative piece. "We have nothing to hide anyhow," according to Paul.

However, I had seen what One Hour could do when on the attack with cameras rolling and I was worried. Could Tanner Energy's environmental record be discussed? Would the discrepancies and inconsistencies in versions of Paul's upbringing be fair game? What about discussions of unproven allegations that Dr. Collin's sons were allegedly stealing JTPA funds? An alleged rape on Loyola's campus and the claim by some politicians that the Louisiana Tanner Plan Legislation was an elaborate hoax were some of my many worries. The claim by some Tanner Kid's parents that the ACT score requirement and "no pregnancy and staying out of trouble" clause was motivated by racism was also a potential problem. Hour One News would not negotiate discussion points before hand and it could be unwise to alert them to our concerns. It is impossible to know with certainty what someone will say since you can never be totally sure of their motivation, like the history of the Ford Motor Company told from the viewpoint of Henry Ford as opposed to a labor union representative.

Our new lobbyist team, including Frank, did not like the idea of doing the Hour One segment, but decided in favor. The potential national rewards were worth the risk. We suffered through many late night practice sessions preparing Paul for difficult questions should they arise. Hour One crews filmed the Tanner Kid's Summer Program graduation ceremony at the University of New Orleans and also the Kid's visit to the Tanner's Foxworth Mississippi ranch. The television crews planned to interview the kids, parents, instructors, and local politicians and condense everything into one twenty-minute segment. Walter Wallace was pacing nervously at the UNO student center, "Where are all the people that are suppose to be here?" he asked.

"Not to worry," I said. Dr. Collins managed to invite half the city and within the next hour there was standing room only. Just as promised.

Paul liked the song "Beneath My Wings" and selected the song as the event's theme. The intended message was with Paul support, these kids could soar higher than an eagle. Dr. Collins invited a Baptist choir from a local church to perform. Paul and Mrs. Tanner were standing hand in hand as the choir in red robes stepped on stage and began performing the closing theme. The singing continued on and on, the improvisation seemed to be empowered by the audience's enthusiasm that moved in waves over the crowd. Hands began reaching high in the air, in unison, voices rang out, "Amen, that's right, thank you Jesus, can I get a witness?" Paul looked awkward, unsure what to do, he stood stiff, like a Republican politician and nodded his head out of time, clearly out of his element around so much emotion and passion. However, the celebration was a spontaneous, unscripted outpouring of appreciation that was emotionally powerful and deeply moving when aired nationwide.

It was the first time out of New Orleans for most of the Tanner Kids when we rented a tour bus and brought them to the Foxworth Mississippi ranch. The Kids dressed the part of tough urban kids and looked intimidating, but the truth was another matter all together. They were unsure and silly around the opposite sex. They joked and laughed but were nervous about leaving New Orleans. They pronounced oil as earl, toilet as tirlit, and when it was necessary to use the bathroom they said they had to go "make." The discussions I overheard included terms like; solid quarter and hose pipe, the very same language I remember as a child in my home.

They enjoyed fried catfish prepared by Tanner's staff and ate hotdogs from Tanner's authentic French Quarter Lucky Dog cart. He was the only private individual ever allowed to purchase one of these unique examples of urban vending art. For what he paid, he could have had a Bentley. We planned long hayrides where the kids got to know the Hour One staff and charmed them with their good natured innocence.

The Tanner kids were goody goodies compared to the badass friends I grew up with. I began to wonder if the "stay out of trouble and avoid pregnancy and drugs" clause in the Tanner Kids college guarantee was based upon unfair stereotypes. One particular Tanner Kid lived in an especially dangerous public housing development with courtyards that prevented easy access. As soon as the van door opened, he always took off running like a bat out of hell. I asked him why. He said he ran so the criminals and drug dealers could not get a clear shot. "They got bad dudes up in there!" He lived with his mother and three siblings, prisoners in their own home, a good kid.

57

PAUL PLANNED A RECEPTION AT the Bilton Library at Lee Circle for the night of the Hour One News broadcast. At one time the monument to Robert E. Lee was the tallest structure in New Orleans. Lee faced North as an eternal reminder for Southerners to remain vigilant. Tanner had the statue cleaned and restored. The restoration crew used crushed walnut shells propelled through a pressurized system that effectively removed years of grime and neglect without inflicting damage. Paul also purchased the Lee Circle, home of the first female attorney in New Orleans, and planned a restoration of the only private residence ever built on Lee Circle. The residence had fallen into a state of serious disrepair and was used as a derelict bar and hangout. Before the purchase, Paul sent me to look around. I entered the bar, walked down a long hallway towards the bathroom and encountered a drunken bar patron relieving himself against the wall. "Why don't you use the bathroom, asshole?" I asked. Without turning his head he said, "Because it's fucking filthy in there."

The greatest real estate prize on Lee Circle was the Brown Stone Howard Bilton Library building, a New Orleans historic landmark. When the law firm that had occupied the building split up, Tanner moved in and acquired the building at a bargain price. Restoration was complicated and expensive, but worth the effort. Paul had stones brought in from the Massachusetts quarry that supplied the original stones. It was here, in the library rotunda with a sandstone fireplace, that Paul held his party celebrating the Hour One News airing.

Seventy to eighty special friends and supporters were invited, but hundreds turned out. I know Paul enjoyed seeing so many New Orleans Blue Bloods at his event. Old New Orleans never accepted Paul; they called him an interloper, not liking his brash manner, lizard skin boots, western suits, or the loaded pistol he usually carried. For his part, he did not like their inherited status and patrician manner. Paul tried to join HEX, the premier Mardi Gras society in New Orleans, a few times, but was rejected without explanation. When the Mardi Gras Krewe faced financial struggle, Paul offered to purchase one of their historic floats for display at the Foxworth ranch. Their reply was, "Mr. Tanner, the heritage of this great city is not for sale. Some things cannot be purchased." Privately they said, "New money, trying to look old is embarrassing."

The historic HEX floats of canvas and paper maché were built on ancient wooded wagons with wooden spoke wheels wrapped in a steel ring that left thin white tracks on modern streets. Floats shook and vibrated as celebrants made their way down St. Charles Avenue. Life in New Orleans has always been difficult, modern construction projects regularly turn-up mass unmarked graves of Yellow Fever victims. The wagons beneath the Hex floats may have been used to collect those disease victims.

The wealthy had summer safe homes in Bay Saint Louis and Mandeville, the poor stayed in the city and died by the thousands. During the worst of the "Yellow" epidemics, wagons rolled day and night, collecting bodies. Trenches were dug at the back of the city; victims were buried quickly, without regard to race or religion. The Bishop stood at the head of each trench sprinkling holy water "ashes to ashes, dust to dust, to dust you shall return." Like so much in this ancient city, even Mardi Gras is a metaphor for life's struggles.

58

THE LOBBYISTS WERE HERE, OF course, protecting their interest, taking credit for everything, and shamelessly trying to parlay their Tanner connection into more business. Mahogany walls of the rotunda were lined with television sets, chairs were added to accommodate the large crowds, and additional caterers were hired. Obviously, we expected a positive story, but the segment was even better than anyone could have hoped. At the end of the broadcast, Paul stood up and raised his hands to the sky. He put his hands down and then thrust them upwards again. Cheers grew louder and louder. Everyone wanted to shake his hand, Paul him on the back, and take a picture with him. The adoring women were not shy about broadcasting their intentions. This was his finest moment. As a courtesy, Paul allowed the Governor a few minutes to deliver a talk about education reform, but no one listened, including Paul. He moved on to shake more hands and greet more supporters.

Building upon the momentum created by the national Hour One exposure "Tanner Plan" legislation was introduced as both a Senate and House bill. The Senate version was designed as a fall back position. The House bill failed to make it out of Appropriations based on trumped up funding concerns. The bill also failed in the House Education Committee. However, we successfully moved the Senate version past the committee hearing almost too late in the session to call for a floor vote. Kissinger used to say that if something happened once it was coincidence, twice was happenstance, and three times was enemy action. I believed our lobbyists were working to defeat the "Tanner Plan" bill. They sold out Tanner in an effort to reintroduce the bill next year once they collected another twelve months at $7,500 each. Like most mercenaries, Frank Bradley had no loyalties and worked for the highest bidder, soldiers of fortune wearing custom suits and wing tip shoes.

I finished a BESE meeting and walked across the grounds past Huey Long's grave to the Capitol Building. The Senate was trying to tie up a few loose ends before the session ended. I sat in the back of the chambers and watched the proceedings. The Senate President sent word for me to come to the podium to discuss the Tanner Plan bill. He explained to me in detail how our lobbyists sold us down the river. "Labor and the AFL-CIO including the Teamsters and Teacher groups want the Tanner Plan," the Senate President explained. "The Governor called this morning and said to pass the Tanner Plan. We can slip the bill on the calendar first thing tomorrow morning. We'll catch everyone with their pants down!"

The Tanner lobbyists watched agenda developments closely and were outraged to discover my last minute trickery. Frank knew once votes were called, no politician would be on record voting against such a popular idea.

Paul arrived in Baton Rouge the next morning to secure last minute support before the vote was called. Frank convinced Paul that this was their plan all along. He pulled me aside, "You have no idea how much money your little stunt just pissed away." He continued, "You should not even be here. This BESE spot was intended for Dr. Demarest. Andre, you screwed that up, too!" Frank explained in a threatening tone. "I will enjoy watching you twist. You're done!" he said while poking my chest with his finger.

"Frank, don't ever touch me," I said with my face an inch from his and my hand locked in a vice grip around his skinny wrist.

He looked away and placed both hands in his pockets. "You y'ats are all the same. I own suits worth more than your education," he said under his breath. "Oh, one last question. Are you all Coon-ass or part nigger, also?"

Paul was granting television and radio interviews and calling the legislation the "Phoenix Bill" because it had risen from the ashes of certain political defeat. The Baton Rouge paper said, "The plan deserves all the support it can get. The educational level of the state's workforce must be raised closer to the national average if this state is to compete in today's complicated, technological world. Providing an incentive to high school students who would otherwise consider further education as an absolute impossibility certainly is a long stride in the right direction." The Senate version of the bill was sent to the House where a floor vote was quickly called with little or no opposition.

A conference committee worked out the minor differences, including the bill's name, officially the bill became TOPS, "Tuition Opportunity Program for Students." Politicians were unable to stop the bill, but did manage a final insult by removing Paul's name, unwilling to risk additional delays, Paul did not object. We immediately began calling it the, "Tanner Opportunity Program for Students." Still TOPS. A final version of the bill was ready for the Governor's signature and then Paul would have his College Plan law. "No student who qualifies will be turned away from college because of a lack of funds," Paul said.

We returned to New Orleans on the Falcon jet with everyone enjoying champagne. "You all have my eternal gratitude as well as that of thousands of Louisiana youths who would have never known the inside of a college classroom but for your leadership and good work." Paul raised his glass. "You can also take pride in the fact that this legislation will keep all children in school, kindergarten through twelfth grade, no matter how much further they go after high school." Frank looked over at me and winked. Paul continued, "Louisiana has made an historic first step." Paul congratulated his lobbyist team for saving the day, promised them a bonus and a position on the Tanner Energy Company Board of Directors.

Graduation and Political Demise

59

I WAS LACKING ONLY A few classes to complete eligibility requirements for the Tulane degree. Obtaining my degree had been a difficult challenge and, foolishly, I postponed tackling the most challenging coursework until the very last. Now, I faced a difficult semester, advanced math, probability and statistics, and challenging economics. I had to finish soon because the legislative battles were winding down and I did not know if there was a future role for me at Tanner Energy.

Like Mt. Everest climbers that turn back short of the summit. They can spend their lives second guessing, wondering if failure exposes inner flaws lesser people can keep hidden. On an early spring afternoon, I was sitting on a bench under an oak enjoying the evening breeze that carried the scent of the season's first azalea blossoms. Tulane University Grounds Keeping Department employees were busy as the campus green spaces were replanted each spring. I watched a worker preparing a flower bed across the sidewalk and complemented his work. He came over and struck up a conversation using imperfect English. Having been a doctor in Bangladesh with a large family that immigrated to America recently, they struggled financially. The children were college age and he did not have the time to earn an American medical license. "Tulane offers free tuition to the children of employees," he said. "This is great job. My children get education." I was embarrassed about the insignificance of my struggle and felt almost like I should apologize because my path was easy by comparison.

Dr. Barrilleaux was waiting in the hall in front of my class. "Nice to see you. I would have called but knew you would be here," he said. Just when I felt overwhelmed, he reminds me of the reasons why I was here in the first place. "Class is starting, only need a minute. I'm proud to say that the faculty and staff of the College have selected you to deliver the Commencement Address at the Spring Graduation Ceremony," he said.

"Selected Me?" I thought about my dad working as a young maintenance electrician around students that were his age at that time. They had opportunity; he had a 9 to 5, a stack of unpaid bills, and babies to feed. "From maintenance electrician to commencement speaker in one generation," I thought.

The Dean must have read my mind, "Don't worry, your dad will have a front row seat."

I took a break from working on the Tulane commencement speech and while reading the paper a small ad announcing an upcoming silent auction held at a neighborhood Catholic elementary school caught my attention. They were seeking donations, auction items. I called the school and they said that the net profit goal was about $3,800. Profits could be lower this year because they rented an inflatable space jump for the kids, a financial leap of faith. "We are praying for good weather and strong attendance," they said. Driving over would be a nice weekend outing, I thought.

I had not driven the Packard in a long time, but it fired up as expected. The V8 engine was smooth as silk, even when cold. I pressed the accelerator, encouraging a speedy warm-up, and oil circulation. As I did so, the powerful torque caused the front-end to slightly rise and tilt as the RPMs increased, exhaust rumbled as the automobile came to life. The automatic garage door opened, I lowered the convertible top and backed the Caribbean out onto the driveway. There is nothing like driving a Packard on the open road, it jumped up to 90mph and was still at just a gallop. Not many people around today can say they drove a Packard at 100mph, but I can! Not many can say they made love in the back seat of a Packard, but that is a story for another day. I loved this car!

My car drew a crowd wherever it went, strangers did not hesitate to approach. "Is that a Packard Caribbean? I always wanted one but in those days a Navy enlisted man's salary didn't go very far." Every time I took the Packard out, it was like a reunion among long ago friends. "Is it for sale?" Even people who were not automobile enthusiasts recognized the special pedigree of this car. Fifty or so people gathered around as I arrived at the school auction.

I found the event organizer, John, actually he found me because he was there in the group admiring the Packard. "What a beautiful machine," John said.

I walked around to the passenger side and opened the glove box, signed the back of the title and handed it to him with the keys. "You teach children. That's powerful stuff." I caressed the hood, careful not to leave fingerprints on the mirror finish and walked away. John was running and leaping into the crowd, excitedly waiving the title in the air and calling for the parish priest. I heard something about completing a library expansion. My conscience bothered me a great deal about keeping the Packard but I felt really wonderful giving it away.

Dave Levet called. I was glad to hear from him, but felt guilty because we had not talked in a long while. Just too busy. He and I had developed the kind of friendship that did not need repeated confirmation, but I know that if I was in a bind in the middle of the night I could call on him. Dave said he was doing fine, but it was the kind of half hearted response you give when the truth is just too complicated for a short conversation. We made plans to meet for dinner in Bay Saint Louis.

The last time I visited the Landmark the wait for a table was thirty minutes and I noticed prices had increased. Appearances indicated that financially things had to be good, but Dave lost a lot of weight and did not look healthy. His face was more red than usual and his right hand shook noticeably although he tried to hide it. "Great to see you Dave. How have you been?"

I put my left arm around his shoulder. "Are you O.K., buddy?"

Without answering my question he requested two vodkas on the rocks. "Forget that; bring the bottle and two glasses with ice. We will be at the back table," he instructed the bartender.

"I'm not a fool, despite what they think." He finished his first drink. "Did they think I wouldn't know why Doreen was always working late, traveling with politicians, dinners and outings, why she was calling numbers in DC?" he asked, but not really expecting an answer. I knew where this was going. "I really don't blame her," Dave said. "After all, I haven't been able to provide in adequate fashion. I don't own airplanes, we don't travel, how could I compete with that? These politicians, they exploited her weaknesses. Frank, he was my friend. I blame all these bastards. They have been here, in my restaurant, drinking with me in my bar! Back stabbing bastards!" He was nearly finished another drink. "We hadn't made love in a long time. Doreen was my wife. They stole her."

"All marriages have their ups and downs, you know this. Could this be just a rough patch, something all married couples experience from time to time?" I asked.

"You are trying to make me feel better. I appreciate that, but this is business now. Doreen is gone, I want revenge."

I hoped he wasn't planning anything stupid. "Dave, it's not worth it. Besides she may come back."

He looked surprised, "Who said anything about taking her back? I don't want her back; I want revenge, to hurt them more than they hurt me." He reached under the table for a brown envelop that I had not noticed earlier. "You will know what to do with this." He slid it across the table.

I looked at Dave, then the envelope. "Open it," he said. I slid two fingers in at the top and opened it wide enough to see inside without removing anything. Inside were a dozen 8x10 black and white professional quality photographs. "I told you, I'm not stupid," he said in a satisfying way. I was not surprised by the graphic nature of the raunchy pictures of Doreen and Lynchard, but was very surprised by photos of Frank and Congressman Lynchard engaged in sexual activity with each other.

These rumors had persisted for years; Congressman Lynchard always seemed to surround himself with pretty young boys, his Beltway nickname was "Congressman Tube Steak," but this was something else all together. "Oh my god! This man will be Speaker of the House. How any Congressman could be so stupid, especially the next Speaker, I wondered. Are there other copies?" I asked Dave. "No, you take them; I wash my hands of the matter," he said.

61

"DAN, WAKE UP, I NEED to see you!" I said.

He sounded really sleepy. "Do you know what time it is?" he asked.

"Of course I know what the damn time is. I'm driving from Bay St. Louis; I'll be there in forty minutes," I said.

"OK big guy, we'll get the coffee going. Be careful!" Dan would know what to do. He opened the door with a broad smile and warm embrace. "Great to see you, I know you want coffee." He asked Camille how the coffee was coming. She emerged from the kitchen wearing a ruby red silk robe with matching slippers, silver earrings and a tray carrying the coffee service.

Camille was Dan's favorite girl, always together. "It's OK to look. I know how beautiful she is," Dan said. "We're both happy to see you."

"Don't pay Dan any mind," Camille said with a slight blush. She looked over at Dan and told him to "Behave, bad boy."

He responded with a devilish wink that, I sensed, carried private meaning. "Well, you sounded very troubled, we were worried," Dan said. "What's on your mind?"

I started to tell the story but stopped, "I should just show you," I said.

I handed him the envelope. "What do we have here? The location of Jimmy Hoffa's body perhaps." He laughed and slapped my knee, the mood changed quickly. "Camille, honey, please excuse us." He said nothing more until she was out of the room. He massaged both temples by moving his head up and down while holding his fingers in place, and then he stood up and paced back and forth. The photos were spread on the table. "Did anyone in the restaurant catch a glimpse of any photos?" he asked.

"This is my ticket to Congress, right?" I asked.

"Andre, this is more important than any single race or individual. Do you realize what the implications of this could be?" He explained, "I mean the possible implications for you as well. This is the next Speaker, current Chairman of the Ways and Means Committee. This could make your political career or destroy you," he said.

"Destroy Me! I'm not in the pictures. How could this possibly hurt me?" I asked.

"Do you think they will allow this to go unchecked, they will fire back with everything, including discrediting the source? In this case, that would be you! Never underestimate what your opposition is capable of!" Dan came up with a temporary game plan.

The Security Center on Gravier Street was originally a Federal Reserve System Bank and was built like a fortress by the Federal Government. Now privately owned, individuals could anonymously rent secure boxes using only numeric identification. Following Dan's instructions, I paid cash for six months and memorized a random six digit code. I did not write it down or share it with anyone. The clerk recorded my code with the number on the security box. The photos were as safe.

62

ALTHOUGH THE TOPS BILL WAS signed into law, the real challenge became controlling the implementation. Many questions arose that had not been anticipated. Can Community College and Technical College students qualify? If the FAFSA form was used to determine eligibility, how would that impact other student financial aid awards? Is there a fee for filing the application? Would TOPS cover summer school expenses? How many semesters would TOPS cover? What about a second undergraduate degree? Would TOPS pay for graduate or professional school? Would students have to re-qualify each year? Can an extra foreign language credit be substituted for a math requirement?

A student born in Louisiana and moved to Italy as a baby now speaks fluent Italian, but does not speak English well. "Can my English classes satisfy the Foreign Language requirement, or can my Italian language skills count?" she asked. "What about high school students that have taken college courses for credit, can these be counted as core required courses?" Or, the eligibility of a Louisiana student whose parents are military officers stationed overseas? Answering these many questions became the work of the staff at the Board of Regents and the Office of Student Financial Assistance. We worked closely with them to protect Paul's vision and defend the original spirit of the legislation.

One simple question nearly derailed everything and it came close to making TOPS just another of the many mediocre financial aid schemes available. "Can TOPS awards be used with other scholarships and financial aid?" A "yes" answer gave Paul his dream. A "no" answer meant that other funds would be subtracted from a TOPS award, leaving most applicants with nothing new. Paul produced a ½ hour TV infomercial describing the Tanner Plan and its purpose. One million dollars in hundred dollar bills was placed on a table watched over by two armed guards. "This represents the difference in lifetime earnings with a college degree," he said. The show aired in most Louisiana cities.

Once these administration issues were settled Louisiana became the first state to offer universal college availability. The enrollment period that first year was cut short due to administration hurdles; nevertheless over two thousand applications were received. Paul always believed that citizens tolerated mediocre education in Louisiana because they believed college was out of reach. Now all of that was changing. Education reform was becoming a grassroots statewide movement. School systems began to see enrollment serge in calculus and integrated mathematic, biology, physics and chemistry enrollments. French, German, Italian, Japanese, Latin, Russian, Spanish and Chinese are now taught in Louisiana public schools.

A uniform statewide grading scale had to be considered since this was the only way to compare GPAs from the different 66 school systems for awarding TOPS scholarships fairly. Without a statewide universal grading scale for the 66 systems, schools may be tempted to lower their scales to get a TOPS advantage. The St. Tammany School Board was the first district to try and beat the TOPS GPA mandates; they implemented the easiest scale in the entire state. The St. Tammany Superintendent said the new scale, "Offers hope to floundering students thinking of dropping out."

The dropout rate was not going to be solved as easily as changing a grading scale. St. Tammany's grade scale change was a blatant effort to secure a greater share of TOPS funds intended for the entire state.

"It is nearly impossible to impose a TOPS GPA requirement if it means something different in each school system," I said.

BESE was divided on the standardized grading scale issue. John said that an "A" in one parish is not the same as an "A" in another. "Every teacher and school grades differently," he said.

I said, "Unified scales would make grades a more reliable measure of student performance."

State Superintendent Culver appointed a commission to study the issue and in a surprise move BESE accepted their recommendations. Under the new system, school districts could continue setting their own grading scales. The difference now is that the scale on which the letter grade was based would be printed on the transcript. "This does negate the incentive school systems may have to lower grading scales in a misguided effort to win scholarships," the superintendent said.

The most controversial new TOPs reform to arise was the Minimum Foundation Program (MFP) equalization plan, because it was seen as helping poor school districts at the expense of the wealthy. How could students from poor districts meet TOPs requirements if their schools could not afford to offer the necessary course work? Should prosperous school systems be penalized because they raised their own taxes to support schools unintentionally creating funding inequality from parish to parish?

The state funded public education at a certain uniform level using the Minimum Foundation Program. A few parishes had successful economies or oil production that allowed them to subsidize the state's minimal education allowance. However, without a special economic windfall, most Louisiana parishes struggled financially. The MFP formula was designed to distribute state funds to local schools, "guaranteeing" a minimal basic education. MFP requires no goals or objectives or spending oversight and certainly no fairness. Louisiana received Justice Department inquiries regarding the fairness of MFP even before TOPS. Challenging the US Department of Justice was never a good idea; thus equalizing funding became a top priority of BESE.

I had seen poor children in Ruston using 20-year old science books, schools in Shreveport with inadequate heat, and elementary schools in Lake Providence with asbestos issues. I traveled to North Louisiana in the dead of winter; a light snow was falling when I arrived at an ancient elementary school in a hopeless neighborhood called the "Bottoms." The 1930's building with large single pane windows was cold; students wore coats all day long, breath vaporized like smoke in the dimly lit hallways. I was greeted by a group of sixth graders walking single file, a young man stepped out of line, firmly shook my hand and asked if I could help heat his school. "Mister, we're so cold!"

With an existing sizable tax base to support schools, St. Tammany voters felt their children attending in a wealthy school system should not be penalized? Jefferson and St. Tammany parish voters taxed themselves to subsidize state formula dollars. Funds raised above a certain level locally would result in a reduction of state funding dollars, creating an equalization mechanism as excess dollars were redistributed to needy districts. Another provision in the new plan would punish these districts further if they refused to tax themselves to prevent equalizations charges. I had seen enough of the hopelessness in the eyes of children around this poor state and believed that worthwhile education is a fundamental right and the state's responsibility. Funding equalization was not a political maneuver, it was a moral imperative.

I worked to pass the funding equalization plan, but the first two BESE votes failed by a small margin. The issue passed on the third ballot by a single vote. I was awarded an Honorary Doctor of Humanities degree from City College in Shreveport. The degree reads; "This degree is awarded in recognition of eminent scholarship, outstanding leadership in the field of education and administration, and great accomplishments in Christian service, and devotion to the highest ideals of patriotism and citizenship." Really cool for a y'at, huh?

63

I WORKED FOR WEEKS ON the Tulane commencement address, but continued to worry that I would not graduate on time. Graduation would be determined by a final exam grade in a single math class, everything else was completed satisfactory my last semester. I was unsure of the outcome when I approach the hall where grades were posted. All my work came down to this moment, years of effort dependent upon one letter grade on one piece of paper taped to a wall. Pass or fail. BESE, Tanner Plan, TOPS were all meaningless to me without this. A Tulane education would mean that my family, from this time forward, would settle for nothing less. A Tulane degree would set a new benchmark. Tulane would become a part of our pedigree, opening new possibilities, and new expectations previously not considered realistic.

The polished floors made the hall appear longer than it actually was, like mirrors on the wall of a small room. I took a deep breath, stood still for a moment, then walked towards the postings. I supported my weight by leaning against the door jam with my left hand, using my unsteady right to scroll down the grades listed under student numbers in no apparent order. The ink was smeared from other students dragging their fingers along just as I was doing. I found my student number and moved my finger across the sheet to the grade listings and briefly closed my eyes. "I did it, I really did it!" I doubled checked to be sure. I thought I was prepared, but the realization that

I would graduate from Tulane University was overwhelming. I leaned against the wall and slid down to a sitting position, where I stayed for a long time.

Tulane prepared an alumni announcement for the commencement ceremony that contained a review of my background, first in my family to go to college, BESE, TOPS, and some hints of the speech to come. The announcement also discussed my family's New Orleans history and generations of struggle and failed to mention my sister held an Associates of Arts in Home Economics. A friend gave her a copy of the announcement. "Didn't you go to college?" she asked. Sis read the article, called Dad and demanded that they go to Tulane and "set the record straight." She hoped that in light of this development, Tulane still had time to select a new commencement speaker and avoid any further embarrassment.

My father said I should not have discredited my sister and that I needed to correct the error with Tulane. "I am disappointed in you. You didn't have to do this at the expense of your sister," he said and hinted that it would be difficult to attend the graduation knowing this.

I did not bother to explain. "Well pops, you do what you feel is right," I handed him the invitation. "Either way, it's OK. I love you, old man."

Each graduating student was allowed a limited number of tickets for friends and family. We arrived early; most seats in the auditorium were already taken, but some up front were reserved for my family. "Commencement Speaker", the signs read. Angela was with me, but I was unsure about anyone else. Standing room only and the first row seats would be empty. I thought about taking down the "Reserved" signs so that others could use the seats and I could be spared the embarrassment. "It really makes no difference if they are here or not. You earned this, it's your night. Go on that stage and celebrate the moment. It will stay with you forever," Angela said.

A Tulane photographer was available to record the event. I treasure the black and white photos with the University President and Dr. Barrilleaux, but I was also worried about the tassel. Should it hang on the right or left of the cap? Everyone on the platform wore it on the left; others I saw wore it on the right. I could not establish any rhyme or reason and decided to keep it on the left since faculty and staff had it that way. They should know, I reasoned. I did not know that if one already had a degree, the tassel was worn on the left, while others wore their tassel on the right. Once degrees were conferred the tassel was moved to the left. My tassel was wrong nearly the entire night. This doesn't sound like a big deal, but academic protocol is very important in these circles.

My classmates lined up first and began the procession into the auditorium. They were happy and carefree, I had butterflies. As I lined up in the designated place, I saw Dan and Camille, "A blue-eyed Creole with a Tulane education, watch out world." He was proud. Camille was crying, she kissed her hand and touched it to my cheek, fighting back more tears. Dan moved my tassel to the correct side. "Knucklehead" he said with both hands on my shoulders. Once the graduates were seated then the faculty and staff, university president, chaplain, I and various dignitaries and important people entered. I followed behind the president, ahead of the chaplain. We walked down the center aisle then turned to the left towards four steps that led to the stage. That turn was directly in front of the seats reserved for my family.

To my surprise, everyone was there. Maw Maw Dupree was seated on the first seat to the right. She was fighting Dementia and now living at my parent's home. Her once vibrant life reduced to one bedroom and a box containing mementoes, personal affects and photos. Father sat next to her, then Sis. She brought with her a copy of her Home Economics degree; it was clinched tightly in her lap. She mumbled something as I walked by. "Shut up. For once, just shut up," Dad told her. Behind them were the Mount Mariah Lodge members. I walked onto the stage and sat between the President and Dr. Barrilleaux, President Kelly welcomed everyone and the Chaplin delivered the invocation. I noticed Dad was wearing his Bolivia watch that he purchased in Japan while in the service; it was his prized possession, only worn on the most special occasions.

I never forgot my sixth birthday and the gift my Dad gave me. To some, it was just a streetcar ride and spending time where Dad worked. To me, the day was magical and changed my life forever. I thought about what my Dad said as I sat on stage, "That building is where Tulane gives degrees; it is the most important of all."

Once the Chaplin was done, President Kelly stepped back to the podium and introduced me. Dr. Barrilleaux gave a nod of confidence, "You have already made me proud," he said. I began by discussing challenge and hardship, the importance of taking risk and overcoming fears. The lights were hot and distracting but I found passion. "It is very tempting to take the easy road. Don't do it! My greatest fear is to become an old man sitting in a rocking chair and wondering what could have been, full of bitterness and regret. I don't want to be like Prince Charles, always waiting!" My eyes were adjusting to the lights and I could now see the audience. I told the story of the man who gets to the gates of heaven and asks Saint Peter who was the greatest general of all time. Saint Peter points off in the distance towards a certain individual. "That man? I know him. He is from my village. He's not a general, he's only a cobbler." Saint Peter then said, "Yes, but he would have been the greatest general for all time, if he had been a general."

"Jackie Cochran was born into poverty, but became the first women pilot to break the sound barrier," I said. "She was told that women could not do these things, that the F-86 Sabrejet was not capable, excuses, excuses. The Air Force forbid it, "Suicidal," they said. On May 18,1953, Jackie flew to 30,000 feet then pointed the F-86 nose directly at the ground and jammed the throttle forward, hitting 652 mph and making history. Never worry about failure," I said. "Worry about the opportunity you miss if you don't even try." My fellow students rose to their feet in applause. Tears ran down my father's cheeks from maintenance electrician to commencement speaker in one generation. No more floodwater fishing for me. I escaped the 9th Ward that night.

64

WE CELEBRATED THE COMMENCEMENT AT Fitzgerald's seafood restaurant at West End, where they once served boiled crabs by the dozen and spicy crawfish by the pound on round plastic trays advertising Falstaff, Dixie and Jax beer. Back then, it was always crowded and noisy. Servers yelled orders to the kitchen, "Oyster po-boy dressed, roast beef sloppy, dozen blues-cracked." Children ran around newspaper covered tables while parents built up mounds of crawfish heads on the Falstaff trays. Today, all the food seems to be prepared by some nondescript distribution company. Fitzgerald's had been my grandmother's favorite. We came back this night as a family to help her remember.

The West End establishments were built out over the water on the Jefferson Parish side of the line; all tax revenue went to Jefferson. In retribution, Orleans Parish fenced the parking areas and began charging outrageous hourly parking rates. In a short period of time, business died off. On this evening, we were the only diners in sight. The kitchen and wait staff spent most of the evening gathered around a small TV watching a basketball game.

Visiting the West End these days was like looking-up an old lover. You may feel tempted, but you know it is probably not a very good idea as memories are best kept unspoiled. Spinnakers had burned down to the waterline and the current owners saw no reason to rebuild, but the sign survived, announcing a vacant space over open water. Arson was suspected, but never proven; it was more like euthanasia. After dinner, I mentioned that I wanted to earn a Master of Economics degree. "Your sister has an economics degree. She can help you study," mother said.

I wanted to explain the differences between International Economics and Home Economics, but kept quiet. "That would be helpful," I said. "Thank you."

I could see the Bounty from Fitzgerald's window; they closed early because there was no reason to do otherwise. A distantly familiar older man locked the Bounty doors and walked to his car, a rusty Trans-Am. Time can be vicious. "Are you okay?" Dad asked.

"Sure," I said and turned away from the window to rejoin the dinner conversation. "Onward!" Monday morning I submitted an application for admission to Tulane's School of Graduate Studies.

65

AT PAUL'S ENCOURAGEMENT, I BEGAN seriously planning a Congressional run against Lynchard. Paul promised to provide the necessary funds and I promised to work harder than ever. BESE elections were every four years, Congress is every two. The BESE redistricting indecision caused an election postponement resulting in unusual concurrent elections. Most politicians seek higher office when the elections are staggered, that way they do not risk their current position seeking the new one. I could not run for both at the same time, it would be all or nothing, "all in" as poker players say.

The fact Paul Tanner declared war against Congressman Lynchard was well known. Paul wanted it that way because he intended to make the Congressman sweat. I began by visiting each newspaper editor in the district, promising each that I would run a clean campaign.

"You're not going to discuss the tube steak thing? That's too bad," said the editor in Franklinton, Louisiana. His advice was to attack, attack, and attack. I promised to purchase a full page ad and he promised his paper's endorsement, hoping to see real political fireworks.

The Slidell, Hammond, and Ponchatoula papers endorsed the Dupree campaign. Lynchard attempted to block my moves by putting a candidate in the BESE race and directing substantial funds to her campaign. She attacked me for trying to move up politically on the "backs of children," using the Education Board as a platform for advancement was 'immoral', according to her slick campaign material. Sometimes when the British navy attempted to capture an objective the captains set fire to their own ships. There was no turning back, either capture the objective or die trying. Like those British sailors, I had no retreat plan.

"Andre, this is Cyndi. I miss you so much. Our time together was remarkable!" Cyndi was my friend from Washington DC. "I hope we can have Long Island Teas together again soon. I miss you so!" she said. "But Andre, I must warn you. I've heard rumors here that the Feds are coming after you, trying to destroy your congressional race. Be careful my love!" She also explained how Lynchard's staff was cooking-up misleading federal complaints regarding the congressional race and initiating IRS audits of my financial backers. "Election Commission Lawyers are filing complaints against you soon," she said. Cyndi offer to provide evidence and proof of Lynchard's involvement but I declined the offer, not wanting to drag her further into this.

Complying with campaign reporting requirements established by the State Board of Ethics and the Supervisory Committee of the Louisiana Finance Disclosure Act is considered extremely important. I carefully reported all BESE expenses and donations as required by state campaign laws as the fines for failing to do so were substantial and the negative press could wreck a campaign, At this point, I still had not officially declared my candidacy for Federal office and Paul had not actually deposited any funds into the campaign accounts. I assumed I was in compliance with all federal legal mandates, until the certified letters began arriving from the Federal Elections Commission FEC. If a person is a candidate for Federal Office (declared or not) and received over $5,000 in contributions or made expenditures over $5,000, then federal reporting is required. I had not done either at this point.

Cyndi was right. Government lawyers determined that I was indeed a candidate for National Office and was therefore in violation of numerous Federal Campaign Laws for missing report dates, contribution limits and expenditure reporting, you name it! According to the Feds, the issue was now a "MUR," Matter Under Review. Any citizen can file a complaint if they believe someone has violated finance laws. The only requirement is that complaints be submitted in writing and notarized. Most violations result in civil and monetary fines, some cases are referred to the Department of Justice for criminal prosecution.

If the Feds believe this system cannot be politicized, then they are naive. Of course, that could be the intent all along. The old Soviet Politburo had a higher turnover rate than the US Congress; our system is clearly tilted in favor of incumbents, Feds will protect their own. In this case, the people that make the rules also sit in the jury box. Copies of the so-called, "Confidential" FEC- MUR letters were obtained by Congressman Lynchard's staff and leaked to the papers, although they denied the allegation. In light of the developing scandal, the local editors said they would need a longer look before committing anything more to my campaign. Setting up a bogus citizen compliant and then leaking it to the press was good hardball politics, I could respect that.

Dan had come under investigation by the IRS. He was suffering through a Life Style audit, the worst micro and detailed of all IRS reviews. "It was like getting a colonoscopy administered by the government," Dan said. "Don't think for one minute that all this is coincidence." He was sounding like a conspiracy theorist, "We are screwing with ruthless people, don't underestimate these bastards!" Two FBI sedans arrived the next morning, blocking his driveway, the agents' retrieved boxes of records from Dan's office. He thought they were really looking for something much more important. "Keep the stock certificates safe!" he told me in a brief phone conversation. "They are negotiable instruments," he said referring to the Lynchard photos. How could anyone know about the pictures, I wondered?

66

MEANWHILE, PAUL TANNER ATTENDED A meeting called by Frank and the lobbyist team where they discussed the deteriorating circumstances regarding my congressional race. I was not invited, but knew Frank would be dealing from the bottom of the deck and was most likely on Lynchard's payroll as well. " You had better get all this under control real soon or I pull the plug. Understand?" Paul said. I did not know Frank was negotiating peace between Paul and Lynchard. The Coastal Environmental Wetlands Levy was to be exchanged for my Congressional race; a classic smoke-filled backroom deal.

Clearly, I was caught in a no man's land between two political titans in close battle, an expendable pawn. Paul claimed that he never committed to anything on my behalf. "It was all a misunderstanding. Andre Dupree is young and eager with an active imagination, but unseasoned. He has done a great job as a Tanner Energy Intern. During these troubled times, the country needs a man of strong wisdom like Congressman Lynchard," Paul said at the press conference where he endorsed the congressman's reelection campaign. Frank stood at his side. While watching the television coverage, I noticed Frank looked directly towards the camera and winked. He knew that I would be watching. Congressman Lynchard placed his arm around Paul and named him honorary chairman of his reelection campaign committee.

Privately Paul said something very different, "What the hell are you upset about Andre? When we first met you asked for two things: A salary and a Tulane education. Remember? I gave you both! It's a square deal!" He was right, but I wanted to know why he lied at the press conference. "The truth, what is the truth? Did you think I would take care of you forever? Was that what you expected?" he asked. "Nothing is more deceitful than truth!" This meant the end of my affiliation with Tanner Energy Company and most likely the end of my political career as well, but in a strange way, I felt honored by causing powerful people great stress, I mattered!

It took another eight years to finish a Tulane Masters Degree; six years of night classes and two years working on the thesis. Although I never was to see Paul again, I also never saw a Tulane tuition bill. He kept his promise, a square deal! Upon completion of the Masters thesis I received a UPS package containing a handmade Italian leather briefcase, a graduation present from Paul Tanner.

67

I DECIDED TO DROP-OUT of the failed congressional race and seek re-election to the BESE seat. The FEC/MUR issue was intimidating, but viewed as just "big boy" politics, something to be expected at this level. Raising money was difficult but not impossible; I had become an effective fund raiser. The problem was I lost the platform. Even the Lynchard photos would not be enough to overcome that handicap. Politicians need a reason to move up, something the voters will recognize as significant, a reason to ask for a promotion. Some politicians build hospitals, bridges or roads, fight wars or make peace. I had the TOPS success until Paul's press conference drove a stake through the heart of my political career.

As chairman of the Appropriations Committee, the Congressman had brought home the bacon for a long time. They say you cannot beat somebody with nobody, he was somebody, and I could offer only promises. Many voters had benefited from Congressional earmarks, contracts, and other programs; they would fight hard in the Congressman's corner protecting their turf. My outnumbered supporters had opaque promises; they would not fight as tenaciously as those who stand to lose position and privilege.

The Congressman's original handpicked BESE candidate was not the only candidate qualified to run in my BESE race. Lynchard also recruited someone with a French sounding name to erode my natural base. These candidates had at least $75,000 each to spend on radio and television ads and since Lynchard was now unopposed in his election, he would have plenty of time to meddle in mine. I expected him to do everything possible to defeat me, but I did not expect it to become an all consuming passion for him.

This time, campaigning felt very different. Although the daily activities were effectively handled by professionals, I missed the enthusiasm of my old college friends. Everyone had families now, job commitments, house notes, and tuition bills, we had drifted apart. This may have been my fault because things I had been doing always seemed more important, although I always thought about them, wondered what was going on in their lives. I saw my old friend, Phillip, at a parade, he seemed thrilled to see me and promised to call, he never did. Dan was up to his neck in alligators and unable to do much, but I did appreciate his financial support. I was worried about his legal troubles.

My campaign managers were motivated only by money and would sell me out tomorrow for two-bits more. They were untrustworthy and I was reluctant to follow their agenda fully. I was a well-known candidate, but had to buy support since the common wisdom was my campaign would be crushed by the Congressman's powerful political machine and Tanner's money. Campaign workers and party supporters were reluctant to affiliate with a likely loser.

In one of our daily campaign planning meeting, I intentionally mentioned that my opponent's name was not really Cajun French as claimed. The name was unusual but authentic; the managers would not know that. At the next candidate's forum my opponent gave a long dissertation about his name's evolution over the centuries. "I am proud of my French heritage. I am as French as Mr. Dupree. No one can argue that," he said. Perhaps, it was coincidence that my opponent brought up genealogy at this time, but that is unlikely. This was clear evidence that someone on my team was informing the other side. The feeling was similar to discovering your spouse has wandered. Do you confront her or remain quiet hoping that the new thrill will eventually wear thin and things will return to normal. Do you allow your emotions to dictate an irrational response or do you move to protect your interest? Like a wounded spouse, I didn't want to lose my investment, but wanted to punish the betrayal nevertheless at the appropriate time and on my terms.

Despite best efforts by my opponents and by Paul Tanner himself, they could not separate my name from the Tanner Plan and TOPS, years of media coverage assured that my name was synonymous with the Plan. Poll numbers had my candidacy pulling 43% in a three person race. Although currently leading, if I got into a runoff my chances of winning dropped off considerably. In a runoff, my two opponents would combine forces, issue endorsements, and call press conferences announcing their alliance. However, many of the groups and organizations associated with education in Louisiana endorsed my campaign as I called in favors wherever possible. I liked politics best when I was out on the street meeting people, pounding the cement; going door to door building grassroots support one voter at a time. My managers say that is a waste of time, "the district is too large for that foolishness," they said. Their advice had more to do with commissions; they received 15% on media buys, but earned nothing extra for following me around while door knocking.

Political media buys usually require cash, especially as we move closer to Election Day. Once the election committee is dissolved or the candidate loses collecting unpaid debts is difficult. Media outlets learned this lesson long ago. The *Picayune Journal's* endorsement interviews were scheduled the following week. "We need to do a $10,000 hard hitting radio buy now," my advisors said. "It will convince the paper that you are not running scared. That endorsement will determine the winner."

I agreed to the expenditure and handed over the cash. Later I listened to the leading stations, but did not notice any difference in the frequency of my air play.

In the interview, the editors asked if I was a member of, "the old boy network," opposed to meaningful reforms. I explained that if they considered TOPS and the Tanner Kids to be "old boy" failures than, yes I was.

"Well we have a letter here from Mr. Tanner claiming that your role was minor. According to his letter, you were considered an intern."

I suggested that they take the time to read their own archives of stories and reach a conclusion based upon the evidence and disregard what Mr. Tanner is now saying.

"That will not be necessary," they said.

My opponent used her interview to hammer the point that I had tried to use the Education Board as a political stepping stone. She brought with her copies of the articles regarding the Federal Election Commission and the MUR issues. The editors took her points at face value, but they refused to give me any slack, the fix was in. I wanted to explain the Wetlands Tax, the congressional race, Tanner and the skullduggery, but did not have any real evidence. These guys were most likely in on the scam anyhow, but without evidence I would sound like a lunatic conspiracy nut. "I appreciate everyone's time. Thank you for your consideration." I said as I packed up my papers and left the meeting. Five years earlier, the paper's endorsement assured my election and now they could take it all away.

The front page endorsement notice of my opponent trumpeted her dedication to school children and the need to "start over" with new reform programs. "It is time for new ideas moving away from yesterday's failures. The situation is too important for us to stop trying. How do we tell children they need to wait four more years?" The rhetorical question made their point. Once word of the paper's endorsement decision was announced the third candidate dropped out and supported my opponent. Congressman Lynchard ran a full page ad with a long list of politicians supporting his candidate. A few of the names were recognized as people I believed had previously committed to my campaign. With only two candidates remaining, there would be no runoff and they had the momentum, poll numbers and organization. Dupree supporters were scurrying about like roaches in the light, looking for cover.

68

THE DUPREE ELECTION NIGHT PARTY would be a small affair this time held at my home with close friends and family and a few other supporters. I did not want the embarrassment of facing a large crowd, if I had to concede the election as expected. I could read polls and knew what the likely outcome would be. A nearly empty ballroom with balloons and streamers swept into a corner, the humiliation of a public concession speech and then the call to the victorious challenger, is a gut wrenching experience. We have all seen this election night ritual, but few have actually been in that dreadful position. Losing an election is the kind of failure that can last a lifetime, difficult to overcome. Defeat on this scale can become a threshold event, because it steals your confidence, self doubt thumps ego creating a vacuum filled by bitterness and regret. I could accept my election night destiny, because I was very lucky in the first place and happy to have made the trip. In a New Orleans cemetery is this epitaph, "They say I didn't get very far, but it was the world's longest trip on an empty tank."

The reality of my situation was hopeless, like a turtle on a fence post. My secret ambition had always been to win a Congressional seat, hold it for a few years, and then seek appointment as a member of the President's cabinet. I never told anyone because it would be interpreted as ridiculous and overreaching and they would have been right, from rising star to political has-been in blinding speed. We watched the election night returns from home with a few diehard friends, Dan and some family, most of the invites were acknowledged with insincere regrets and creative excuses.

Early returns placed me in the lead, but things changed for the worse as Jefferson Parish results were reported. Someone brought champagne that I opened, pretending to celebrate impending victory, but fooling no one. I hoped they would take the clue and leave early. My opponent was interviewed for television from her victory celebration; the report was cut short because the cheering crowds, band and noise made discussion impossible. I called her to concede the race and offer congratulations, but she refused the call.

Not really sure how to describe these feelings, but recognized the pain. Years before my girlfriend was ill so we canceled a date. Later, I decided to drive over and check on her well-being, discovering that she was out on a date with another boy. Was it the feelings of loss or feelings of rejection that hurt most? Were all those people on TV celebrating someone's victory or my defeat? What had I done to deserve such treatment?

"Andre, I wish I could have done more to help," Dan said. "But you know, Tanner is right, you got what you wanted." I wasn't really sure what he meant. "I'm not talking about Tulane, although that is wonderful. I'm talking about a thorough understanding of human nature, that's real education. After all this, that's the top prize, the brass ring, your education," he said. The final election results were closer than expected 51% to 49%. A loss is still a loss. I felt embarrassed, not for myself, but because I let so many people down.

69

SOON THEREAFTER, CONGRESSMAN LYN-CHARD EMERGED upon the national stage as a leader of the majority party holding key positions and the chairmanship of the Appropriations Committee. The new Republican Speaker Newt Gingrich was credited with creating the new majority and was mentioned as a likely Presidential candidate. The Speaker moved very fast, checking off items from a list created for the first 100 days. If he became a Presidential candidate, then Lynchard would be his likely replacement as Speaker.

But Lynchard began a campaign to replace the Speaker too soon and was viewed as a back stabber. Many on the Hill said what the Congressman was doing was unseemly, and threatened the party's agenda. Sixteen Republican committee chairmen signed a letter to that effect. Lynchard said, "The horse is out of the barn. Once the race for Speaker begins, you must get your votes lined up as quickly as possible. If you don't, you likely won't be in the race." He continued, "I will support the current Speaker as long as he wants to be Speaker and I will support him for President as well. This is not intended to undercut anyone; I am just saying that if he leaves the Speakers office, I'm interested in taking his place."

The Speaker's agenda included closing down the Federal Department of Education, cutting funding for National Public Radio, the arts, the United Nations and many other programs that he viewed as wasteful. The assassination of an Israeli head of state required a top level delegation representing the US at the state funeral. The Speaker was invited to travel aboard Air Force 1, but the Democratic President required the Republican Speaker to enter the plane from the rear. When he publicly complained, he seemed petty and the news media carried the issue as a top story for weeks, thereby eroding the Speaker's credibility. Lynchard used this opportunity to begin opposing the Speaker in public, questioning his ability to lead. The Majority Leader and the Majority Whip also entered the race trying to divide Lynchard's support. Lynchard would need the support of 114 of the 227 Republicans to become Speaker, difficult to do in a four man race. To an outsider, party leadership appeared in a state of insurrection, with Lynchard viewed as a moderate and "healing agent," not the destructive force that he actually was.

President Clinton was under investigation by Ken Starr for lying before a grand jury investigating the Monica affair. The President repeatedly denied involvement with the young intern until evidence proved otherwise. Congressman Lynchard demanded the President's impeachment for perjury and immoral behavior and he attacked the Speaker as politically weak for not driving the impeachment issue harder. The Speaker was unable to maintain support while under attack by the Democrats and leaders of his own party at the same time. Lynchard was named House Speaker-designate and began meeting with world leaders including Yasser Arafat, Tony Blair, and others. He began naming new committee chairmanships, punishing the former Speaker's allies and consolidating his hold on power. He named Frank, Chief of Staff.

70

I ANSWERED THE PHONE.

"Ready to nail that hypocrite bastard?" Dan asked. Life after the election loss was uneventful except for an appointment as president of a hospital board and working on the Masters Degree, which kept me occupied. However, I was tired of being submissive, tired of hiding out, eager to attack. Like lying on the floor of the drug store when the shots rang out, I survived, and emerged stronger. My election was lost, but I was now in a position to help bring down the Speaker of the House, funny how things work. "The Governor is expecting you at his private law office tomorrow for lunch. Bring the pictures," Dan said. "The Governor will ask if you want anything in return. He would be disappointed if you asked for something as simple as money, be creative! That's up to you. But when you attack the king, you have to kill him! Remember, no mercy. I think you are going to enjoy this." Dan concluded.

I arrived at the Governor's private office early as I did not want to keep him waiting. We changed lunch plans and headed over to Chili's, a less visible location. "There are two requests I would like you to consider," I said to the Governor. "First, your support for the Coastal Environmental Wetlands Tax and your influence with the Louisiana Congressional Delegation to pass it," I said and started to explain, he stopped me.

"Andre, I know of your history with Mr. Tanner, explanations are unnecessary," he said. "Next is the matter of Frank Bradley. I want the bark peeled off that bastard." I said.

"Revenge can seem so very sweet; but don't play this game forever Andre, the odds always catch up. That bitterness will eat you alive! Andre, if you sit along the river banks long enough, eventually the bodies of your enemies drift by." the Governor said.

Many bodies have since floated by and I am here writing. In Louisiana, politics is a blood sport. Friends are temporary as long as they serve some useful purpose, enemies are for keeps. The arena floor of Louisiana politics is littered with the corpses of hopeful rivals, the idealistic and fallen kings. The winner stands above the political carnage raises a sword and proclaims, "I am Pontifex Maximus." Until they fall. Meanwhile the disenfranchised continue to sit along the river banks and wait as they have for generations, like Evangeline waiting for Gabriel who never came.

We finished lunch. He hugged the waitresses, while I waited. The short ride back was occupied with discussions concerning blue crabs. "When blue crabs are caught, you place them in a bushel basket and they all fight with one another trying to climb out. But each time one is close to escaping, all the others work together to pull him back in. Watch out for blue crabs," was the Governor's advice. We drove to the office parking lot. "Well?" he said.

I knew what he wanted. After a long pause and a nervous deep breath, I walked around back and opened the trunk, looked over my shoulder twice, removed the raunchy Congressman Lynchard photos from a leather case and handed them to the governor. Thus, the final act of my short and unlikely political career was done.

71

THE FIRST INDICATION THAT LYNCHARD knew of the existence of the photos came after a routine press conference when he surprised the media with a previously unannounced closing statement. "I have on occasion betrayed my marriage." He took no additional questions and quickly exited the room. A famous publisher of porn magazines said that four women had come forward claiming to have enjoyed sexual liaisons with the Congressman, but could offer no real proof. Rumors of a tape of Lynchard engaged in phone sex being in the hands of the publisher emerged and the publisher took out newspaper ads offering $1 million dollars to anyone who could produce real evidence of an affair with Lynchard.

The downfall took only three days. Lynchard met with the Republican Whip and discussed a possible resignation, but continued to pressure the President demanding Congressional impeachment hearings. "No, Mr. Speaker, I will not resign, but you should."

Lynchard's reply to the President was "OK." He then returned to the Capitol Building and made an official announcement on the House Floor, "I'm resigning."

True to his word, the Governor and State Inspector General launched an investigation ferreting out political corruption at the highest levels of state government. There was a moving van in front of Frank Bradley's house. He left the state after his lobbying business failed and he was named a "person of interest" in the far-reaching state investigations. He maintained his innocence and claimed that the prosecution was a politically motivated "witch hunt." Charges were eventually dropped, but his reputation was destroyed and his finances consumed by legal fees. Frank's career came down faster than a prom dress.

Dr. Barrilleaux left his beloved Tulane University after receiving the cancer diagnosis. He spent his last months serving as a Deacon at St. Joseph's Catholic Church. I was sitting in a pew for the 7:00 AM service when he realized that I was there. After mass, we embraced. I thanked him for the influence he had on my life. He died a short time later.

The Tanner Kids finished high school, most "stayed out of trouble, and maintained a 2.5 GPA and completed foreign language and math requirements," but Paul did not "see to it" they would go to college, as promised. He reasoned that the TOPS program would provide all necessary assistance and, furthermore, his efforts to introduce the state plan absolved him of any further financial obligations to the Tanner Kids. Their lawyer claimed that the "Kids" relied on the promise and suffered an injustice, because they reasonably expected Paul to keep his word and act accordingly.

Paul's skilled legal team said it was an illusory promise containing no commitment by Mr. Tanner. "Mr. Tanner's original Livingston Middle School speech was so insubstantial as to impose no obligations on him. His emotional expression of college availability hopefulness seemed cloaked in promissory language, but actually contained no enforceable commitment by Mr. Tanner," the attorneys said. The judge ruled in Paul's favor. Paul would have been named, Ambassador to Ireland, had the Democrats not retained the White House.

Dave, Dan, and I divided the $1 million paid for the pictures, the largest share went to Dave who settled his divorce and paid the Landmark Restaurant off in full. He has since remarried and opened a second restaurant called the "Blue Crab," where we meet to discuss politics and enjoy a few drinks. The first toast is always dedicated to Lynchard. "To Congressman Tube Steak! God Bless!"

Dan used his windfall to settle his IRS troubles, but had enough left to purchase an original Walter Anderson seascape. He married Camille. I was the best man.

I used my share to help support the Pelican Association, a Tulane Scholarship Fund honoring Dr. Barrilleaux and I purchased a small beach house in another state where I now enjoy a quiet life.

The TOPs program is a huge success with thousands of Louisiana kids attending college under the plan each year. Twenty-five states have enacted very similar legislation. Although my political career was short-lived, the ideas live on. Not bad for the Creole son of a 9th Ward electrician.

THE END